TIDE OF UNCERTAINTY

Gill's uncle leaves her the family house and a share in his boat-building business, but should she leave London to live in a sleepy Devon seaside village? Two men influence her decision — cousin Graham, who has made it clear she will be unwelcome, and Pete Oakridge, her closest childhood friend, now even more attractive than she remembers. Always one to take up a challenge, Gill moves down to Devon, but finds that people are acting mysteriously . . .

CHRISTINA GREEN

TIDE OF UNCERTAINTY

Complete and Unabridged

LINFORD
Leicester

First published in Great Britain

First Linford Edition
published 1998

The right of Christina Green to be identified
as the author of this work has been asserted
by her in accordance with the
Copyright, Designs and Patents Act, 1988

British Library CIP Data

Green, Christina
    Tide of uncertainty.—Large print ed.—
Linford romance library
    1. Love stories
    2. Large type books
    I. Title
823.9′14 [F]

ISBN 0-7089-5401-4

Published by
F. A. Thorpe (Publishing) Ltd.
Anstey, Leicestershire

Set by Words & Graphics Ltd.
Anstey, Leicestershire
Printed and bound in Great Britain by
T. J. International Ltd., Padstow, Cornwall

This book is printed on acid-free paper

1

Gillian Wayland saw her cousin Graham the moment the train stopped at Shelmouth Station and knew, immediately, that she wasn't yet ready to meet him.

The funeral she had travelled south to attend was timed for three o'clock — that gave her half an hour to walk along the beach and arrive at The Lookout without having to suffer Graham's patronizing and probably unfriendly remarks. Even after being away for six years, Gill still shrank from her cousin's remembered unpleasantness.

In the throng of passengers leaving the train, it was easy to avoid him and slip into the car-park unnoticed. She pushed her bag into a handy taxi. 'Take this to The Lookout, please. It's at the end of Harbour Lane.'

The driver, little more than a boy,

shock-haired and with merry eyes, grinned. 'No need for directions. I know where The Lookout is all right. Hey — you're Gill Wayland! Come home for the old man's funeral, have you?'

'Yes, I have,' Gill said, hoping her brief, tight smile would stem the flow of local gossip she suspected to be hovering on the brink of the boy's tongue. 'Could you tell them that I'll be there in a quarter of an hour? I need some fresh air rather badly.'

'Looks to me as if you need a lot more than that,' the young driver commented with a disarming twinkle. 'I remember the year you were Carnival Queen — oh, a real doll! Now you're as pale as an oyster, thin, too . . . '

'Thanks,' Gill said, wryly. 'Nothing like compliments to make a girl feel good.'

'Sorry. But I had a real crush on you in those days.' He started up the engine, then gave her another mischievous grin. 'Married yet?'

Her answering smile faded, and for a second the image of Jeff's face was a painful reminder of their recently ended relationship.

'No,' she answered shortly. 'I'm not. And I don't intend to either.'

'Sensible girl. OK, OK — ' as Gill's eyebrows arched with growing irritation. 'I'm on my way. You'll find the fresh air you're looking for down on the beach. First turning left — '

'I haven't forgotten the way.'

'Right.' The car drew away, but the boy's voice wafted back to her, saucy as ever. 'If you're home for good you'll need some proper gear. London clothes won't get you anywhere in Shelmouth, you know — ' Tyres screeched and Gill smiled recognizing youth's need to impress.

As she headed for the main road she recalled who the driver was — young Ian Robinson, an impish page-boy tugging at her Carnival Queen gown all of eight years ago. The smile grew as she remembered other faces, other voices, and gradually her city tension began to leave her. Oh, yes, it was marvellous to be back . . .

The thought became a certainty as, recalling Ian's advice, she gave up the idea of walking in high heels on the golden, crunchy sands below the promenade, and contented herself with gazing out to the far line of the waning tide, where a hazy foam of breaking surf decorated the long, stretching beach.

If high heels and tight city skirts were not suited to this quieter, more rural way of life, neither was the stylish haircut, now being blown out of shape as the offshore wind roared up, slapping her about with cheerful gusto.

Gill walked on towards The Point, at the estuary end of the prom. All around the familiar sights of childhood met her eyes, reassuring her that nothing had changed. Until she recalled the reason for being here, and the greatest change of all — Uncle Harry was dead.

She sighed, and felt her mood sink lower. The beach was as lonely as usual in winter, windswept and bleak, with only a few hardy dog-walkers dotted along its length. Scurries of gulls were blown overhead, their mournful cries yet again reminding her of the funeral to come. She braced herself sharply, walking on quickly, pulling her cream tweed coat closely about her body.

Death was a part of life and Uncle Harry had been a vital, happy man, who would never have wanted her to grieve unduly at his passing, at the ripe age of eighty-seven.

By now she was approaching the little cut of road that turned the corner leading to the sheltered harbour, facing north and away from the slapping wind coming off the sea. In less than five minutes she would be at The Lookout, the large family house standing beside Wayland's Boatyard, the business started by her great-grandfather in the mid-eighteen hundreds. Very soon she must explain to Graham exactly why she had chosen to avoid him.

As if conjured up by her thoughts, suddenly he was there, glaring out of his immaculate F registration Jaguar as he braked sharply beside her, leaning across to shout from the passenger window, 'Knew I'd find you skulking around the beach; just like you to cause trouble the minute you arrive. Didn't you see me at the station? Honestly, Gill . . . '

Swallowing the quick anger that his familiar grumbling called up, she managed to smile sweetly at him. 'Sorry, Graham. But I had to get some air after that over-heated train.'

'I suppose that makes sense — but you might have waited till you saw me . . . well, hop in. I'll drop you at The Lookout and then go and pick up Aunt Mary.'

Gill said quickly, 'No, I'll walk — that'll save you an extra journey, won't it?'

Her cousin's plump, rather petulant face relaxed slightly.

'Right. See you soon, then.' He

revved the engine, then shouted further instructions. 'Don't be late, Gill. And I hope you've brought something dark to wear. Father would expect it, you know.'

Gill watched the opulent car purr silently away, and reflected rather grimly that Graham was the same as ever: bossy, humourless and utterly lacking in understanding of everybody, including his own dead father. Uncle Harry, with his cheery attitudes and warm compassion for the remainder of the world, would never have cared what she wore to his funeral.

She turned into Harbour Lane and was soon at the sturdy, black-painted gate of The Lookout, and the closed front door faced her. Gill frowned. In Uncle Harry's day the door had been ever-open, come rain, sun or storm.

Instinctively she tensed, lifting her hand to pull at the old rope-supported ship's bell that hung in the porch, and waited, wondering who would appear to let her in.

'Yes?' The middle-aged woman opening the door stared, unsmiling, her one word a query sharpened by obvious irritation.

'I'm — I'm Gill — Mr Wayland's niece . . . ' It was quite ridiculous, having to explain herself. Who on earth was this hard-faced stranger who sighed, stepped back, saying curtly, 'Well, you'd better come in. Graham's gone to meet you. Did you miss him? He'll be ever so cross.'

Gill controlled her flaring annoyance and disbelief. She saw her bag standing in the hall and said, rather coldly, 'We have met. He knows I'm here. If you tell me which room I'm to sleep in tonight I'll go on up and get out of your way, Miss — er — Mrs — '

'Rachel Campion. Mrs.' A grudging smile showed disinclination to be more than merely businesslike. 'I've been your uncle — your late uncle's housekeeper for four years now. You'll be in the little room at the back. Excuse me, Miss Wayland, but I've got a lot to do.'

'Of course. I'll go up and get ready. Graham said he was bringing Aunt Mary here. I'll be down to meet her.' Gill picked up her bag and retreated, feeling Mrs Campion's critical eyes following her as she went.

★ ★ ★

The small room at the back of the big, rambling old house was no longer the chintzy, nursery-like bedroom she remembered with affection, the room she had moved into after Dad died, when she came to live with Uncle Harry and Graham. Now it was anonymous, with insipid, shabby curtains and ugly furniture.

She sat down on the bed with alarm and growing despondency. And only a few moments ago she had been telling herself that nothing had changed.

Then a gleam of winter sunlight suddenly shafted through the small window that looked out over the harbour, and Gill got up with a spurt of new hope. At least the river and the distant landscape must still be the same.

As she stood there, wistfully exploring the familiar scene before her, her eyes widened. A small boat came out from the nearby slipway of the boatyard, gleaming and newly painted, its classic lines reminding her of the happy days when Dad was alive, and a new boat was christened before being sent out on trials.

As she watched the craft chugging along, her mind focused more sharply, and the old, unthinking knowledge she must have amassed as a teenager came into the forefront of her mind. She noticed that the boat had none of the trendy innovations common nowadays in small craft, and was glad of it. Waylands had always been famous for their old-fashioned, elegant lines.

There were two people aboard and she could see them clearly as the boat smoothly chugged past her window. A man with bright, tousled hair, and a girl dressed in an eye-catching scarlet anorak and matching pants.

The girl's sultry, dark charm and animation caught Gill's attention, but then her mind was turned back to the man with the fair, blown hair; an unforgettable memory surfaced, and she knew it must be Pete Oakridge, Uncle Harry's protégé, and a vital part of her own past here in Shelmouth.

Graham's shout up the stairs returned her to the present, and she turned guiltily, calling back a reply as she did so. 'Yes! All right — I'm just coming . . . '

In the hall she found Graham impatiently looking at his watch. He was smartly dressed in a dark, expensive suit and black tie, and raised an eyebrow at her cream coat, but she forestalled any further complaint by saying quickly, 'Is that Aunt Mary in the car? How lovely to see her again . . . '

Aunt Mary greeted her warmly. 'It's been so long, Gill dear. Nearly seven years? Why haven't you been back before?'

'I worked abroad for a long time, Aunt Mary — I'm sure Uncle Harry must have told you. I did write regularly to him at first. But once I got back to London my job became very demanding, and — and I'm afraid the letters stopped — '

Aunt Mary nodded and her faded eyes swam. 'I expect I've forgotten. He would have told me. But we were all growing older, Gill my dear. Ah well. I'm going to miss Harry so much — '

'And me, Aunt Mary — oh, what's that?' As Graham switched on the ignition, Gill heard a hooter in the boatyard blast out.

Aunt Mary whispered, 'That means they've stopped work, as a sign of respect. Graham said it wasn't necessary, but I understand the older men insisted. Harry would be pleased at that.'

Gill watched Graham's grim expression

in the mirror. She pressed her aunt's hand. 'Of course he would. It's a lovely gesture. I'm so glad the boatyard hasn't changed, Aunt Mary.'

'Not changed?' Suddenly there was a harsh note in the quiet voice, and Aunt Mary's hazel eyes burned with quick indignation. 'Don't you believe it, Gill. The way Graham's going on at Wayland's, things will soon be as dead as poor Harry . . . but there, I mustn't say such things. Not here. Not now.'

Gill met Graham's furious eyes in the mirror and quickly changed the subject.

She was thankful when the funeral was over, and she followed Graham back to the car, with Aunt Mary on her arm. The service had been simple but sincere, and Uncle Harry's warm spirit had seemed to be with them. Gill had realized then just how important it was to her to be back in Shelmouth, even though only for a day or two. Roots, she thought, suddenly, aware, roots matter so much.

About to climb in beside her aunt, she became conscious of a man behind her. Turning, she saw it was Pete Oakridge. She frowned, then smiled. 'You weren't at the church?'

'No. Had a client to deal with. Business has to go on. How are you, Gill?'

'I'm fine, thanks.' She recognized that Pete was as taciturn as ever, that he seemed older, leaner, and somehow more strong and silent than she recalled. She wondered how deeply he had suffered when his father, Jack, was drowned in a Wayland's boating accident, and saw the deep lines etched at the sides of his blue, sailor's eyes. So Pete knew about unhappiness and the loss of a loved companion; just as she did, first with Dad dying, and then Jeff walking out on her.

But it wasn't the time or the place for such thoughts. 'We'll have to get together later, Pete. So much I need to catch up on . . . ' Then she was beside Aunt Mary in the car and

Graham was leaning over the front seat, looking pressurized and grim.

'Look, do you think you could fuss over Aunt Mary and the others when we get back to The Lookout? I've got someone extremely important to see, and I've kept her waiting too long already.'

Gill nodded. 'Of course I will. I'll make your excuses. Say you've got something better to do.' She couldn't help the caustic remark, and enjoyed the abrupt surge of colour in Graham's pasty face.

He glowered at her. 'Don't start needling me, Gill,' he snapped, and slid the car into gear as if he was venting his anger on it.

Mrs Campion and a local girl served sherry and refreshments in what used to be the cosy living-room at The Lookout and which had now become an unfriendly, refurnished waiting-room for visiting clients to the boatyard.

Gill settled Aunt Mary in a corner with a couple of old friends, and then went from group to group, introducing herself and trying to make amends for Graham's absence.

By the window she recognized Fred Hooker, one of the old hands in the yard, who greeted her with obvious pleasure and explained that he was recently retired. Garrulous as she remembered, he seemed pleased to have someone fresh to chat to.

'Things've changed, Miss Gill,' he confided, self-importantly. 'Not like it were when your dad and Mr Harry run the yard between them. All friendly then. Now, well, Mr Graham's taken over, see, and he's a real hard'un to please. An' all these new ideas! Can't see 'em catching on. I mean, Wayland's was always known for classic lines — nothing wrong wi' 'em still, I reckon, but he says them's old-fashioned. So he's trying to make luxury cruisers or some such . . . well, that's progress, I dessay.'

Gill had been so absorbed by Fred's confidence that she was unaware of another figure approaching. Now a deep voice added a comment. 'Maybe things won't be as bad as you fear, Fred,' and looking around she discovered Mr Hartland, Uncle Harry's solicitor and friend, beside her. His long, lined face smiled with pleasure as he acknowledged her greeting.

'I'm delighted to see you again, my dear. You've been away too long. Your uncle missed you.'

Gill's face fell. 'I should have come back before. I knew he was slowing up, but didn't realize it was so serious.'

'He wasn't ill — not in that way. And he wouldn't have wanted you to come and fuss over him, not Harry. He went the way he hoped to go — playing a round of golf on a Saturday afternoon, his beloved business wound up for the week, the sun out, and the tide ebbing. An easy end. You mustn't blame yourself for not being here, Gill.'

Suddenly she was threatened with tears, for the first time. Now she realized just how much Uncle Harry and all he stood for really meant to her. After Dad died he had become a father-figure. And now he was gone. Something in her life would always be diminished because of that.

Mr Hartland asked quietly, 'You'll be returning to London, to your job, I suppose, once this is all over? I gather you're happily established up there. Your uncle mentioned a young man in the offing — '

The old-fashioned term helped her to swallow her emotion, and say, with composure, 'I have a very good job, yes. I'm a personal assistant to a firm of restaurant consultants with branches all over the world. And no, I don't any longer have a young man. We split up several weeks ago. It — it wasn't going to work, after all . . . '

'I'm sorry. But you're young and — if I may say so, my dear — extremely attractive.'

Gill chuckled. She'd always liked Mr Hartland, with his well-bred tact and diplomacy. 'Thank you,' she answered airily. 'And, as I think you're implying there are plenty of other good fish in the sea, I expect I'll meet Mr Right one of these days.'

He nodded. 'Of course you will.' A quick glance at his watch, and she saw the professional mask drop back over his face. 'And now, I think we should go into your late uncle's office and read his will. I imagine Graham will already be there, waiting impatiently.'

They exchanged smiles, and Gill knew Mr Hartland quite understood her own appreciation of Graham's complex character. She turned to the old man who had been listening to their conversation. 'Lovely seeing you again, Fred. Hope you enjoy your retirement.' His pale-blue, faded eyes looked at her with sharp assessment, and his calloused hand held hers very firmly. 'Pity you gotta go back, miss, just when you've come, like . . . '

★ ★ ★

19

Gill sat beside Aunt Mary, with Graham at one end of the big leather-covered desk, Pete opposite him, and Mr Hartland sitting at Uncle Harry's swivel-chair with his back to the wide window. She closed her mind to the memories which his figure, etched against the backdrop of sky and harbour, engendered, and concentrated instead on his smooth deep voice as he read the will and explained its contents.

'To you, Mrs Winters, your brother left half his capital. I've jotted down the amount, and the interest it brings in its present investments.' He passed a slip of paper to Aunt Mary, who flushed and put on her glasses, then he continued impassively, 'The other half is left to Graham, his only son.'

Quickly, Gill glanced at Graham, to see a look of satisfaction slide across his face. No more than he expected, she realized, and then berated herself. Of course he expected his father to split the estate fairly between only surviving sister and son; why not? Then Mr Hartland's voice interrupted her flow of thoughts, as she heard her own name mentioned.

'And to my dear niece — almost my daughter — I leave my house. The Lookout, and all its contents, knowing they will be safe in her hands.'

Gill gasped. 'Oh! But I never expected . . . '

She heard Graham clear his throat as she bit off the words, looked at him, and saw immediately that he hadn't expected any such bequest, either. He met her eyes with an almost comical expression, a clear mixture of disappointment, resentment, and then growing, slow acceptance.

'Well, good for you,' he blurted out at last. 'You've always loved the ramshackle old ruin, I know. Personally, I far prefer the house I've built myself up on Marine Drive.'

Gill nodded. Marine Drive was famous for its affluence and position, not to mention the trendiness of its inhabitants. She could just imagine Graham there, in an architect-designed structure, all chrome, plate glass and sea views.

Well, if that was what he wanted, he was welcome to it. She had always felt at home at The Lookout, and even rundown as it now was, it would always have that feeling of warmth and serenity that a proper home should have. Fancy Uncle Harry leaving it to her — she bowed her head, only to hear Graham add, almost mockingly, 'Of course, you'll have to do it up before you can sell it — hope you've got some savings stashed away, Gill.'

But Mr Hartland was continuing. 'And now we come to the disposition of the business, Wayland's Boatyard.' He put the will on the desk and paused a moment before adding, rather more seriously. 'You'll all remember, of course, that Harry's whole life was bound up with his beloved yard, so it's only natural that he gave much thought to the matter of its future once he was gone. Well, his allocation of the total shares of the company is as follows . . . '

Gill sensed a tightening in the atmosphere of the quiet room, and felt Graham shift in his chair, the better to watch Mr Hartland as he went on reading.

'Fifty per cent of the shares to Graham, my son. Thirty-five per cent to Gillian, my niece, and the remaining fifteen per cent to Pete Oakridge, whom I have always thought of as my adoptive son.'

The bare facts dropped into a silence that was more evocative than any words could have made it. Gill gasped and looked first at Pete, whose tanned face gave a sudden surge of colour and then as rapidly died. Then she glanced at Graham. He too was pale, but the pleasure that was Pete's clear reaction was entirely missing from his face.

As Gill watched, fascinated, yet horrified, Graham stumbled to his feet, looking at Mr Hartland and saying, in a rough, almost threatening manner, 'I don't believe it! He couldn't do this to me! Why, the yard was always going to be mine — he as good as said so.'

'Sit down, Graham. No point in getting so worked up. Your father made this will nearly eighteen months ago, and confided in me that he split the division of the shares on purpose.' Mr Hartland was cool and businesslike. 'I know you and Harry had many differences of opinion about the way you saw trade developing. He didn't always agree with your ideas. So he made this allocation of shares in the hope that, with the help, and advice of your fellow shareholders, those same innovations might be tempered and channelled into safer, and perhaps, more conventional outlets.

'After all . . . ' The solicitor raised his voice as Graham began to protest, firmly forcing him to remain silent. 'After all, Mr Oakridge has worked all his life in the yard, as his father, who was general foreman, before him did; he has a background of expert knowledge and experience which must be of help in the future. And as for Miss Wayland . . . '

'She knows damn-all about boats! I refuse to accept that she's going to tell me how to run the business — *my* business.'

Graham's face was mottled with rising colour, and his eyes raged. Gill said coldly, 'I have no intention of telling you anything, Graham. If you'll just calm down, then we can discuss this sensibly. I have no interest in the business, you see — my own job is far too demanding.'

Suddenly Mr Hartland was looking at her over his half-glasses, eyes razor-keen. 'Your uncle asked me to give you this letter.'

Gill opened the envelope, her heart starting to race and her eyes barely registering what the words meant. Uncle Harry's bold back scrawl floated in front of her, and she thought she could hear him speaking. *Dear girl. I'm sorry to put you into what I imagine will be a difficult and awkward situation. I know Graham, you see! But please do as I ask. Remember that your dad and I pulled this old business together by sheer hard, determined work.*

Come back to Shelmouth and help keep Wayland's Boatyard on an even keel. You and Pete must see that Graham doesn't wreck all we've worked for and dreamed about for over half a century.

Please, Gill, my girl, if you ever had any feelings for your old uncle and your dad, do this for us when I'm gone.

Gill's eyes were filling and her voice husky as she put the folded letter into her bag. She looked at Mr Hartland, meeting his searching, slightly quizzical eyes. 'I'll have to think about it. It's such a shock — I never imagined myself coming back here. Or working in the business.'

'Don't worry, you're not going to! I never heard of anything so damn ridiculous! And as for Pete being a shareholder — well, that's just a laugh. I'll buy him out at once.' Graham was blustering again, the old confidence by now putting a smile back on his face.

Gill turned her head sharply and saw the exchange of looks between her cousin and the tow-haired man who sat so quietly on the far side of the desk. She recognized determination settling on Pete's still face, and caught her breath, waiting for him to answer Graham's rude, mocking comment. He took his time to reply, and she remembered that when Pete said anything it was always worth listening to. As it was now.

'You couldn't ever offer me enough to buy back the shares your father has just left me, Graham. I look on this bequest as a trust — and one that I'll do everything in my power to carry through. He wanted me to help run Wayland's. And so that's what I intend to do. Sorry, Graham, but that's how it's going to be, whether you like it or not.'

Graham collapsed into anger again. 'You creeping impostor! So, all those years you were going behind my back, working on the old man. He must have been senile to be taken in by you! Well, I shall contest his will. I shall — '

Mr Hartland cut in very sternly. 'There's nothing you can do, Graham. Your father was most certainly in his right mind when he made these bequests. I suggest you try, instead, to honour his memory by accepting his wishes and making the best of things. Now — there are a few small, personal bequests to members of his staff. Let me see . . . '

Gill heard no more, for her mind was caught up in the dilemma in which she now found herself. So she was to become mistress of an old, run-down house, and a minority shareholder of a business in which she had no interest, save that of loyalty and childhood nostalgia.

Added to that was the uncomfortable pressure of realizing Uncle Harry had relied on her to give up her job in London, her comfortable flat, her circle of friends and interests, and return to small-town Shelmouth, where she would inevitably fight with Graham and become little more than a mediator between him and Pete.

The situation was impossible. Unthinkable that she could do what Uncle Harry had asked; demanded, almost. Her head whirled, and she was torn between frustration, anger and self-pity. What was she to do?

★ ★ ★

She was thankful when Mr Hartland finally folded the will and signalled that the reading was at an end. 'Thank you, Graham, but no, I cannot stay. I have a client awaiting me at the office.'

Gill was about to follow Aunt Mary into the drawing-room, where Mrs Campion had laid the large, gate-legged Georgian table for a traditional Devonshire tea, when the solicitor touched her arm. 'Miss Wayland, if ever I can be of any help . . . '

Her heart warmed at his smile. 'That's kind of you. I might well need all sorts of advice. Right now I'm in a spin. You see, I already have a job that I love, a flat on mortgage, and a lifestyle I don't want to change. I feel like opting out of the situation and selling my shares . . . '

She stopped, seeing a flicker of disappointment in Mr Hartland's eyes. 'After all, darling old Uncle Harry has rather hit me below the belt, don't you agree?' she went on. 'In a way he's putting a kind of emotional blackmail on me.'

Mr Hartland stood up. 'Only you can make the decision, Miss Wayland. As I said before, if you feel in need of advice please don't hesitate to contact me.' He paused. 'You will be hearing from me very shortly, once probate has been granted, with the deeds of the house and transfer of the share certificates. Goodbye, Miss Wayland.'

He bowed, old-fashioned and straight-backed, and Gill watched him head for the waiting car in Harbour Lane before she joined her aunt and the other guests, for tea. Bleakly, she regretted his going, and even more, wished she hadn't been so outspoken.

Graham, she discovered, was at his most charming, and already in a far better mood from that he had displayed only a short while ago. As she entered the large room he came to her at once, grinning in the way she recalled, and making her instantly wonder what he was up to now.

'So there you are, Gill! Thought you'd run off with old Hartland. Hardly the age for you, though, eh? Suppose you've got a chap up there in London, have you? Trust you! Look, this is Brigitte Leconte, she's flown over from Paris to see our boat which was on display at Earl's Court Show a couple of months ago — M'mselle Leconte, this is my cousin, Gill Wayland.'

Gill smiled at the beautiful girl who

confronted her, realizing at once the reason for Graham's change of face. 'Hi,' she said lightly, as recognition came. 'Didn't I see you earlier, out on the water? With Pete Oakridge?'

The lustrous dark eyes smiled back at her, widened, and then glanced flirtatiously towards Graham. Brigitte shrugged and said, with a most charming accent, 'With Pete — oh, yes. A nice boy. Poor Graham was too busy to come.'

Graham snapped up the bait and Gill heard a return of the familiar petulance in his voice as he explained, just a shade too forcibly and uncaringly, 'I told you, Brigitte, I had to go to my father's funeral. I mean, I couldn't help not taking you out myself — well, you know better than that, surely . . . and anyway, we'll take *Melinda II* out again tomorrow, just us, on our own.'

'Oh, no. I will not be here tomorrow, Graham. I fly from London first thing in the morning. You have forgotten?'

'But I thought — you said you were

staying . . . ' Graham was increasingly annoyed, and Gill watched, fascinated, as the French girl cleverly charmed him into a better mood.

'*Chéri*, don't be so cross! I shall be over again soon, like I told your Pete. My father will want to see *Melinda* himself, before he buys.'

'Of course.' Graham made a big effort to calm down. 'Well, I shall look forward to your return. Now — how about some tea?'

Gill was ignored as he escorted Brigitte to the table and fussed about her. She watched his clumsy flirtatiousness with wry amusement, sensing that the French girl easily saw through his efforts, and was sharp enough to perceive the mercenary, ambitious man beneath the light façade.

Then a quiet voice at her elbow said, 'You haven't changed, Gill. Still standing by and watching others make fools of themselves.'

She swung round and looked up into the deep blue eyes of Pete Oakridge.

He was smiling down with the same cool amusement she recalled; his words were thoughtful as ever and to the point.

A great surge of reassurance engulfed her, and for the first time that day she felt something was going right. She and Pete together again, their minds in tune, and the world made more sane and liveable because of their shared understanding.

'Oh, Pete, thank goodness you're here.'

'That's nice. And a mutual relief.' His smile broadened.

Mrs Campion appeared beside them. 'Won't you sit down, Miss Wayland? The others are having their tea.'

'Oh, yes, thank you.' Gill waited until the housekeeper had gone, then she caught Pete's amused eye. Cautiously looking around the table she saw Aunt Mary in conversation with an old friend, Graham concentrating on Brigitte, and the other guests involved with one another. No one seemed to be missing Pete and her.

Mischievously, she touched his arm. 'Quick, let's get out.'

As they had done so often in childhood, when adult occasions grew too fussy and demanding, so they now fled, escaping by the back door of Uncle Harry's study into the boatyard.

★ ★ ★

Legs dangling happily over the high harbour wall, they shared the same hard-worn stone that had so often in the past been a secret meeting-place. Beneath the wall the tide steadily flowed. Overhead, a party of foraging gulls screamed around a returning fishing-boat.

To Gill it seemed that the years had been peeled back. She looked at the quiet man beside her and smiled, ruefully discovering that he was watching with the same intense awareness she remembered so well.

'Come on then, Gill, let it all out, just

what you think of Graham's grumbling and growling. I could see you were amazed.'

'Pete — ' She paused, looking away upriver to where the hazy shadows of distant moorland mingled with the clouds of approaching darkness. 'I can't do it, you know, Can't come back.'

'But your uncle wanted — ' Then he stopped, and she knew that he had never believed it right to try to make people bend to his will. He wouldn't do so now. She sighed; in a way she had almost hoped he might. For if she had someone to argue with she could make out a good case about not doing as Uncle Harry wanted. And then she wouldn't feel this terrible guilt.

The wind blowing in with the tide suddenly seemed chill and piercing. Gill shivered and immediately Pete was on his feet again, pulling her up with him. 'I shouldn't have brought you out here. It's getting late and it's cold.'

'No — wait a minute — before you

go — ' She paused as he opened the door into the house, wanting another few precious moments before the cloying demands and responsibilities closed around her again. Taking a deep breath, she turned and looked down the length of the boatyard.

In its emptiness and silence, the shapes of docks and gantries and passageways created a fantastic world of dark and shade beside the swiftly-flowing, gleaming river. As her eyes absorbed the physical shape of the old yard, so memory's ear recalled the sounds of it. Saws. Drills. A gamut of voices, with gentle Devon burrs and occasional laughter. And then the smells — spicy fragrance from sawn timber. The deep harshness of tar. And over all the pervading salt smell of the sea.

This is a haunted place, thought Gill, a wonderful place. How can I possibly leave it to Graham. To change — to destroy, even?

Pete's hand on her arm made her

turn again. 'Gill, come inside — '

Sighing, she followed, letting him close the door behind her, and black out the clinging past.

* * *

After Devon's clean air and green spaces, London seemed even more grimy, noisy, and claustrophobic than usual when she returned next day.

The train journey over, she spent a couple of hours at her office dealing with important messages, and then told her secretary she'd be in first thing in the morning.

At home, the flat's understated elegance and comfort did little more than make her remember what had happened to The Lookout and again force her into realizing she was its new owner.

Restlessly, she wandered around the rooms, touching her favourite pieces of bric-à-brac, admiring the water-colour of old London Bridge Jeff had given her for a birthday present. She told herself adamantly, this is my home. I feel right here. I could never settle anywhere else. Certainly not in a remote, dead-end small fishing town . . . the Gill Wayland who loved it as a child is grown up now. A different person.

Late in the evening she sat down with a new novel and a glass of white wine, hoping to free her mind of the mêlée of conflicting thoughts that still filled it. Resolutely, she told herself that tomorrow she would write to Mr Hartland and tell him she had decided to sell The Lookout.

When the telephone rang, she paused before answering it. Few of her friends rang at this hour. Instinctively her mind flew to the one person who had always wanted to chat before bedtime when he was away from her. But she and Jeff had broken up. Why should he ring now?

Her voice shook. 'Hello? Who is it?' She let out a deep intake of breath with a mixed sense of disappointment, relief and suspicion, as Graham announced his identity.

'What do you want?' she asked sharply. 'It's nearly midnight — I'm just going to bed.'

'Don't bite my head off, Gilly!' He had only ever called her that when he wanted a favour. 'I've got news for you.'

'Oh?'

'Still angry with me, then? Well, I don't blame you — I wasn't exactly bursting with pleasure at the news but I've got used to it now.'

'So what do you want to tell me, Graham?' Past experience rang warning bells in her head. He was being charming, helpful, and apologetic, and that wasn't really Graham. Which meant he wanted something. He was intent on playing a game. She must be very careful.

'Simply that I've found a possible buyer for you.'

She didn't understand immediately. 'Buyer? What for?'

'The old house, silly. The Lookout. He's even keen to buy it as it stands, ramshackle ruin and all. How about that? Talked of an amount that made my hair stand on end; you'd be a fool to turn him down, Gilly.'

Gill's business acumen took over. Cautiously she made her voice easy and pleasant. 'Mmm — sounds interesting. Perhaps I'd better come back and discuss the matter. Who's the man, do I know him?'

'No. A friend of a friend. No need to come all the way to Shelmouth, though, Gilly — I'll tell his solicitor to contact you. It can all be dealt with that way.'

He didn't want her down there again. He simply wanted to get rid of all possible interference from her, in both his life and his business. Get rid of The Lookout first. Then force her — somehow — to sell her shares. The same with Pete. And then the boatyard would be his completely.

Gill smiled. An incisive note entered

her voice as she said serenely. 'I'll be down this weekend, Graham. See you then.' Quickly she replaced the receiver and then returned to her novel and the half-finished glass of wine.

But no sooner had she entered the living-room than she knew. She would meet this challenge with all the strength and courage she was capable of, because Graham must be stopped, as Uncle Harry had asked. And her first move in this dangerous, unsettling decision was to move into The Lookout.

She would put this flat on the market first thing tomorrow morning.

2

It was raining when the train deposited Gill at Shelmouth Station on the following Monday, and she quickly accepted Ian Robinson's convenient taxi service. She listened, amused, to his facetious chatter about coming home yet again, but knew a feeling of increasing indecision as he left her in the foyer of the Hotel Mirabella on the rain-drenched promenade.

'I'd like a single room for a week, please.'

Now that she was here she discovered her angry determination to thwart Graham's tricks was fast waning. Had she been an impulsive fool in putting her London flat on the market? Thank heavens she had merely taken a week's leave from her work, not yet put her resignation on the line, which had, at first, been her intention. Shelmouth in the rain on a grim winter's day did not, after all, seem as attractive as it had last week when the sun shone and childish nostalgia exercised itself.

Gill looked bleakly out of the window from the first floor of the hotel and watched thundering grey waves breaking along the wide curve of sodden beach below her, grimly accepting that she had been too emotional in her decision to return.

She sighed. Well, it would do no harm to spend a few days unwinding. Her job as PA to the managing director of Fermoy Restaurants Ltd was demanding, and she had taken no leave since that last disastrous trip to the South of France last summer with Jeff.

Jeff — for a painful moment she recalled how close they had been. If only they were still together now he would advise her, console her over Uncle Harry's death, and the problems that his bequest were causing. Then she forced away all thoughts of Jeff. It was over. She was alone and must deal with life by herself.

Later, changed and refreshed, she left her room, heading downstairs for the little bar in the corner of the spacious, centrally-heated lounge, prior to having dinner and then an early night. She had a feeling that the next few days would be busy and stressful.

A figure entered the foyer as she ran downstairs, letting in a gush of cold air and a flurry of rain. Glancing down, Gill was immediately delighted to see Pete Oakridge's direct blue gaze.

He shook himself like a wet dog before taking off his anorak and grinning at her. 'Thought you might like to see a friendly face. Drinks time, is it? Right then, what'll it be, Gill? Vodka and blackcurrant? Or have you grown out of such childish things?'

Gill had a sudden warm feeling as her tension faded. It was just like Pete to come as soon as he knew she was here — what a friend. Happily, she said, 'That was a long time ago, that vodka business. I'd like a dry martini, please.'

'And a lager for me.' Pete smiled at the attentive woman behind the bar. Then he looked at Gill with a wry expression.

'I suppose you know the grapevine is humming madly? All Shelmouth knows you're back. But why, they ask themselves — come to stay, have you? Going to cause trouble? Rows with Graham, newfangled feminism causing chaos and strikes at the chauvinistic boatyard? I tell you, Gill, no one will be watching Dallas tonight, they're all too busy making up their own version of the Wayland story.'

Gill cupped her glass, smiling at him over the rim. She felt relaxed and safe. What did it matter if she had made a stupid move, leaving her flat? She would ring in the morning and cancel the instructions to sell. No harm was done. And it was great being here with Pete, imagining the town gossips doing their worst . . . he was her almost-brother again, just as he had been in their shared childhood. She wasn't alone while Pete was here.

'Let them talk,' she said complacently. 'To tell you the truth, Pete, I haven't reached any real decision myself — not yet. I needed a holiday and here I am — it's as simple as that.'

She wouldn't say anything about the flat and her first, impulsive decision. Tonight she needed a carefree, relaxed chat, picking up old threads of companionship. The future could wait.

She looked at him closely, drinking his lager, and noticed again the unfamiliar signs of maturity on his tanned face. Her thoughts turned to his father's tragic death, and before even thinking of how he might react, she said quickly and sympathetically, 'I read about the accident, Pete — about Jack's death. It was in all the papers, of course. I should have written, but — well, I was caught up in my work, just about to fly off to the States, and you know how it is . . . '

She saw a shadow invade his face, turning the eyes dark-blue and cold. Her heart fluttered for a second. Had she said the wrong thing?

Pete put down his tankard and straightened his wide shoulders, no longer looking at her, but inspecting his hands, now laid impassively on the bar in front of him. 'Thank you,' he said carefully, and was silent.

The awkward moment went on too long. Wildly, Gill sought to make amends. 'I'm so sorry, I shouldn't have said anything. But I thought — well, it's nearly a year now — I hoped you'd be feeling better about it by now . . . '

Pete lifted his head, looking at her with a strangely anonymous expression on his face that caused a prickle to run down her back.

'Of course. And I do,' he said slowly. 'I've got used to Dad no longer shouting at me for lying in bed in the morning. Not having him about the cottage, all pipesmoke and untidiness. His fishing-gear under my feet. Not hearing him cough; watching him smile; wondering how a man like that could have just sunk and died, instead of swimming to shore when the boat went down under him . . . '

Gill heard the cool words grow impassioned and bitter until he snapped the last one off. Dismay filled her. She hadn't thought that Pete could feel like this — that he hadn't been able to accept that his father's death was the accident it had been reported to be.

'Wh-what do you mean?' she asked warily, and watched how Pete's eyes grew large and hard.

'I mean that he needn't have died.'

'But the paper said that Graham tried to rescue him. Only the sea was so rough Jack was washed away before he could reach the lifebelt Graham threw . . . '

Her voice faded. Pete was staring at her with a look on his face that scared her. He looked as if he might do something terrible. 'Pete,' she said sharply, 'what is it? What's the matter?'

'I — ' For a long moment he closed his eyes before looking back at her. Then, thank goodness it was the old Pete again grinning sheepishly. His hand came up to cover hers and his subdued voice was warm and apologetic. 'Sorry,' he said. 'I've been too much on my own lately. Thinking too much, imagining things.'

Relief swept Gill's alarm away. 'Well, I'm here now, so you can just think about something else for a change. Like taking me in to dinner — how about it?'

His eyes twinkled reassuringly and Gill breathed more easily. It had been foolish of her to talk about Jack's death; obviously Pete's grief was still too raw for him to see things straight. She reminded herself that in their shared childhood, accidents had always been more traumatic for Pete than for her and Graham.

She must remember that, for all his

apparent strength and stoic endurance, Pete was vulnerable. A great wave of protective affection swept through her. 'Come on then, slowcoach.'

Smiling, she led the way into the dining-room and heard his footsteps behind her. It dawned on her once again, as in earlier years, that she was leading and Pete was following . . . quickly Gill silenced the small murmur in her head that suggested such dominance was unnecessary and, indeed, uncalled for. She was simply looking after Pete as she had always done. He'd never complained before. Ridiculous to imagine he might do so now.

★ ★ ★

The meal was a great success. Clearly the Hotel Mirabella chef was a talented cook. Gill smiled over the candle-lit table at Pete as their plates were removed.

'Coffee in the lounge?' inquired the

waitress and Gill said at once, 'Yes, please, by the fire.' Then doubtfully, she recalled that niggling small voice and asked, meekly, 'All right by you, Pete?' and was relieved when he nodded.

'Fine. Then I'll have to be off. Monday tomorrow, and I'm not on holiday like you are.'

Gill sensed a question in the casual response. 'But I'm not going to be lazy, you know. I — I thought I'd go and poke around in The Lookout.'

Watching Pete's expression change, she added defensively, 'Well, it's my house — or it will be. Surely I can go?'

'And upset Mrs Campion? Not to mention Graham?'

Gill felt herself flush. Irritation grew. She let Pete lead the way back to the lounge and settle her in one of the armchairs by the log fire. When the coffee arrived she tried to change the subject, but he said quickly, 'Gill, tell me the truth, are you back for good or not?'

Just for a moment she hesitated, still wanting to keep her options open. But there had never been any pretence between her and Pete. So she replaced her cup on the table and sat up straighter, tensing herself to meet his reaction, her mind suddenly and unexpectedly made up.

'I — I think I'm staying, Pete. But I'm not a hundred per cent sure.'

She thought his face relaxed a little, and was encouraged to continue: 'I mean, I've got to think about giving up my job, which is a good one.'

'Couldn't you still live down here and do it? Get a transfer nearer home?' Pete's suggestion made sense. A glow of subdued excitement began to creep through Gill's body. A strange sensation. Something to do with the way Pete looked and sounded.

Breathlessly, she said, 'I don't know, I might even take up Uncle Harry's advice and help Graham run the boatyard . . . ' And then she laughed nervously because everything was happening too fast, and this new feeling between herself and Pete must be broken before it became too much for her to deal with.

'Don't look like that!' she chided him. 'I am a shareholder, you know! Graham couldn't stop me if I really did want to go into the business.'

'I'm a shareholder, too, Gill. Only a minor one, but — '

'Of course! Maybe we ought to get together and tackle Graham. It would be just like old times again!'

Pete smiled, but shook his head very positively. 'Old times are past, Gill. Things can never be the same as they were. We're all different people now, with new ideas, new attitudes. Don't fool yourself into thinking you can just step back and press a magic button.'

Gill stared, her face sombre. He was right, of course, and she had been naïve and stupid to even think otherwise. She looked away from his watchful, intent gaze, feeling uncomfortable. Their relationship was no longer the easy one of childhood adolescence, she realized it now. They had grown up. Grown apart.

Something deep inside her diminished. But the next moment her customary optimism and determination came flooding back. She lifted her head defiantly.

'Perhaps I have been thinking just that, Pete. But I see you're right. And so I'll take it from here. If I do decide to stay, it won't be because of childish longings for past happiness — or people' — momentarily Pete's eyes narrowed — 'but because I can see there's a job that I would enjoy doing, in congenial surroundings. And that's all.'

They looked hard at each other, and Gill knew she had said the right thing. No longer would he consider her a foolishly nostalgic girl, creeping home because of half-baked romantic illusions. He must know now that she would come back to Wayland's Boatyard as a career woman, intent only on furthering the business to its full potential.

* * *

Monday dawned fresh and newly-washed after the weekend storms. Firmly Gill put aside all thoughts of relationships, concentrating instead on jobs and houses. She walked the length of the lonely promenade directly after breakfast, feeling more at one with the weather and environment in her jeans and anorak than she had done in her city clothes last week.

The Lookout stood in full sunshine, its chipped paint and bleary windows shining like banners of defiance in the merciless morning light. Gill saw cracked tiles on the roof, a bulge in the corner of a wall, and rotting timbers beneath a bedroom window-frame. She guessed Uncle Harry had been too concerned with the state of his business to worry about minor repairs to his old home.

Well, she would have to get them put right before she sold the house. *If* she sold it. For a second she imagined the shabby building had a vulnerable look about it; forgotten, neglected. She tightened her lips. So much for sentiment. The Lookout was merely a house in disrepair and she would find a builder this very afternoon.

Mrs Campion was, to say the least, put out by Gill's quiet and polite insistence on entering and inspecting the house. She stood in the doorway with annoyance etched deep on her plain face. 'Graham didn't say you were coming; no, not a word — '

'I don't suppose he did. But I'm here, Mrs Campion, and I'd like to look around, please. After all, the house belongs to me now.'

'Well, really! I don't know *what* he'll say . . . '

'And I don't care very much. Please let me pass, Mrs Campion — '

The altercation was unpleasant and unnecessary, but Gill managed to ignore it. She spent a good hour going from room to room, making a list of everything that needed repairing, and was thankful that the task took away from her mind all the sadness of childish memory. Emotion, Gill decided, was one thing she could well do without; the problems facing her must be resolved by clear, logical thinking and nothing else.

But her own clear thought was hard-pressed when Graham appeared later in the afternoon. She was sitting in Uncle Harry's swivel-chair, deep in consideration of the finances of necessary repairs, when Graham threw open the door and strode in, exuding obvious annoyance.

He glared across the desk. 'And what exactly d'you think you're doing here?'

Gill kept her temper. 'Adding up sums, actually.' She forced a smile. 'Come on, Graham, don't be so heavy! Uncle left The Lookout to me, remember? So I thought I'd come and see the state it's in. After all, you did say you'd found a buyer for it.'

She watched his visible effort to control himself. 'Well, of course.'

'And I told you I was coming down when you phoned on Saturday — so why are you surprised to see me? Try to understand that I'm a big girl now, Graham. I do as I want, not as I'm told.'

Their eyes caught and a silence built. Graham's grin was weak and he said, too heartily, 'My word, Gilly, you *have* grown up! You sound quite a man-eater. Not the dear little soul — '

' . . . you used to boss around. No.' Gill recalled Pete's wry words. 'People do change, you know, Graham. I'm quite different now.' She paused, then added sardonically, 'Are you?'

His dark brows met in a shaggy line and he turned away from her saying crossly, 'I haven't got time to play games, Gill. I just want you to understand that I need a decision.' Abruptly he swung around to face her again. 'Are you selling The Lookout, or not? If you are, then I've got to find new offices.'

Gill leaned back in her chair. She imagined how Uncle Harry must have sat here, many times, while Graham tried to browbeat him, just as he was now. The thought gave her fresh impetus. Briskly she made a final decision and said, 'I shan't sell. I'm going to live here myself.'

Graham was dumbfounded. His colour came and went and Gill saw his hands clench into fists. For a second she had a crazy notion that his rage was so great he might well throw himself upon her.

The thought forced her into movement, and she pushed the chair aside, scraping it warningly on the floorboards. 'You'll have to find those new office premises, I'm afraid, Graham. Unless you'd like to rent some rooms from me.'

Perverse pleasure grew as she watched incredulity dawn on his set face. 'I suppose you could have the dining-room and the little utility room beside it. I shall enlarge the kitchen and eat in there — so I could spare those two rooms for you. I'll ask Mr Hartland to draw up an agreement, shall I?'

By now, Graham's breathing was noisy and his eyes sent off sparks of fury. Then he slowly restrained himself, turning away and heading for the door. He laughed, a feeble, over-forced sound, and said bleakly, 'OK, I get the message. But I'll need time to think it over. I'll be back to see you tomorrow.'

Gill waited until he was halfway through the doorway before playing her trump card. 'Fine. I'll be here. Oh, and Graham — remember to bring your keys, will you? You won't need them from now on. But I will.'

★ ★ ★

The next evening, Pete appeared again in the bar of the Hotel Mirabella, and

Gill was surprised at her pleasure in seeing him. They sat side by side while she told him of her decision, and she waited eagerly, a little tentative, for his reaction.

'I see.' He drank his lager very steadily and didn't meet her eyes.

Just that. No sharing of her enthusiasm, no reassuring smile to make her feel she was doing the right thing.

Gill felt anger grow, unreasonable, but urgent. She sipped her Martini fiercely, looking away from him, and began to wonder, after all, if living here in Shelmouth would work. Then, slowly, her doubts faded, to be replaced by a growing irritation and belligerence.

Facing Pete, she gave him a hard stare and said aggressively, 'You think I'm wrong. So tell me why?'

Pete's blue eyes were abruptly full of amusement. 'I'll do no such thing. If you want to live in the draughty old Lookout, then you'll do it and nothing I can say will stop you. You never listened to me before, why should you now?' The blue eyes softened and his mouth lifted. 'I tell you what, though — I know someone who might be a likely lodger for you. You won't want to be alone in that creaky old ruin; never did like spiders or spooks, did you, Gill?'

Again he'd taken the wind from her sails. Despite her annoyance, Gill couldn't stop herself grinning weakly back at him. 'Don't worry, I'll have The Lookout thoroughly modernized, so that there won't be a chance of finding either.' Curiously, she added, more gently, 'What do you mean, a lodger?'

'I know a young girl called Lindsey Angus. She's a student doing a cookery course at Torquay Technical School. She lives next door to me and is keen to get away from home. You're both cooks, you'd get on well together. Shall I suggest she comes to see you?'

'Hold on. I haven't said I want a lodger yet!'

'But you do.' His eyes were firm. He'd always been the one to try to earth her scatterbrain ideas. 'So I'll see Lindsey tomorrow evening. Maybe she could come round here with me . . .'

Gill paused. She saw the logic of his advice, but resented such dominance. 'Getting to be quite a regular caller, aren't you, Pete? Are you sure your local harem won't be jealous?' She had the satisfaction of seeing momentary confusion cloud his clear-blue gaze.

'Women don't bother me,' he retorted, and she knew she'd scored a goal, despite his quick denial. Wickedly she enlarged on her success.

'Of course not. But little Lindsey somebody next door is hardly *women*, is she? Come on. Pete, stop looking so sour! So you fancy her and it'd be more convenient visiting her at my place than under the watchful stare of her disapproving parents!'

With a stab of unexpected dismay, despite her flippancy, she saw how a quick expression of relief lightened his face. Suddenly she couldn't take any more. Let Pete live his own life and fancy whoever he chose — it didn't matter one little bit to her.

Sliding off the bar-stool, she looked at him coolly. 'OK. Bring her along tomorrow, if you like, and we'll discuss the idea. But I make no promises. Well, I'm hungry now. I've had a long day. If you don't mind, I'd like my dinner . . . '

Gill ate a lonely meal and discovered during coffee, that despite the excellence of the food she had not really enjoyed it. Her bewildered mind was churning too fast with thoughts of first Pete, and then his unknown girl, Lindsey, to concentrate on anything else.

★ ★ ★

Graham appeared at The Lookout next morning as Gill was tidying out Uncle Harry's desk. She heard his footsteps crunching along the passage but was too intent on her task to stop. Only when a hand roughly pulled her aside and snatched away the pile of files she held did she swing around to angrily face him.

'Leave this desk alone — all this belongs to me, not to you.'

Gill looked at him coldly. 'Correction,' she said acidly. 'They belong to the business, actually, and the boatyard is thirty-five per cent mine. So I have every right to handle them.'

Graham glowered, his face set and heavy, and she saw how the fleshy crease between his brows formed a deep vee, emphasizing the frustration in his eyes. With a feeling of pity, she realized that the annoying boy she recalled had become a power-motivated, near-obsessional businessman. For the first time since deciding to move back to Shelmouth, she knew a moment of reluctance.

Graham seemed so intent on ousting her and keeping the business to himself that she wondered how far he might go — surely he had enough self-control to handle the admittedly awkward, but not impossible, situation?

Perhaps he read her thoughts. Suddenly he left her side, marching to the window and staring out at the harbour. When he spoke his voice was quieter and more friendly.

'So you've decided to take up Father's suggestion of becoming involved in the business, have you? But what about your job in London?'

Taken aback, Gill played for time. 'I'm on holiday at the moment. There's no question of leaving . . . ' She watched as he turned, looking at her with a calculating expression. 'I mean — well, I haven't quite decided yet . . . '

'Let me know when you do. If I've got to put two more desks in my office I'll need some notice. Type, can you, Gill? Bookkeep? Work a computer? It'll be quite a comedown, won't it, after your high-flying PA job?'

She could deal with sarcasm easier than the previous raw anger. She smiled. 'Oh, I'm not just a pretty face, Graham. I can turn my hand to quite a few things. And talking of offices reminds me — may I have those keys? I asked you before, remember?'

A mottled flush spread over Graham's vexed face. Alarm touched her again, but even so, she was unprepared for his reaction.

Swiftly and with a sense of barely-suppressed rage, Graham pushed a hand into his jacket pocket. She saw the keys briefly gleam in the light before he threw open the window, raised his arm and tossed the bunch away.

They both saw them fall into the pounding waters of the harbour. Graham looked sideways at her. He smiled with immense satisfaction, like a small boy who has just won a petty argument, and leered at her.

'Oh, dear. So sorry,' he murmured. 'Can't think what came over me.'

Somehow, Gill swallowed her own fury. She knew she must keep calm, whatever happened. That was the only way to deal with Graham's jealousy and possessiveness. She forced a smile on to her set face.

'Never mind, I've got my own key. And no doubt there are others somewhere around. At least, I know that particular bunch are no longer in *your* pocket.'

Silence built as they looked at each other assessingly. Then Graham shrugged, buttoned his jacket and turned away. 'Let me know what you finally decide to do, Gill,' he ordered.

She watched him leave, delaying her answer until he was in the passage. 'I'll give you my decision before I go back to town on Sunday.' Her words echoed hollowly in the quiet room. Graham's crisp footsteps slowly faded and she was alone again.

Taking a deep breath to calm her racing heart, Gill sat down in Uncle Harry's old chair and thought, hard and long.

★ ★ ★

When Pete duly arrived in the hotel foyer at his usual time, he was alone. Gill raised her eyebrows, quick to mock in order to hide her own surprising feelings. 'No Lindsey? Has she turned me down as a landlady without even saying hello? How ungracious.'

Briefly, Pete ran a finger down her cheek. She was uncertain if the movement was a caress or a reprimand. 'You're far too quick on the draw,' he said pleasantly. 'Sit down, relax, and let me explain.'

She sank on to the stool rather heavily. What with Graham's anger this morning and now Pete's ambiguous attitude, she felt decidedly weary.

Pete ordered the drinks then gave her a shrewd look. 'Sure you know what you're doing, back here in Shelmouth, Gill?'

Instinctively, her chin lifted. 'Certainly. Don't lecture me, Pete. Things are difficult enough without that.'

'You and Graham had another tiff?'

She nodded. 'You could call it that. He loathes the idea of me being here.'

Pete fingered his glass, looking away. 'Have you asked yourself why?'

Gill opened her mouth to reply, but he cut in quickly before she could say anything. 'Oh, yes, I know the obvious reason — he wants to run the yard his way, without interference. But he's being unnecessarily nasty about it. Why, I wonder?'

Gill frowned, then smiled. 'Graham's always been nasty. This is nothing new.' She caught the expression on Pete's pensive face and her smile died. 'You mean there's something else? Other than the business? Another reason for not wanting me — or you, come to that — to become too close? Too involved?'

Pete wouldn't meet her curious gaze. 'I didn't say that,' he hedged.

'But you hinted at it.'

He drained his glass, then his face lifted into a reluctant smile. 'Don't let's get all worked up. There are other things to life besides dear cousin Graham.'

'Like Lindsey?' The name slid out unthinkingly and she saw him withdraw into the well-remembered obstinate anonymity.

'Of course,' he said clearly, stone-walling. 'Like Lindsey. She phoned to say she had to stay on at school. Couldn't make it tonight. Maybe the weekend, she said.'

Gill felt strangely defeated. 'I'm going back on Sunday.' Her voice was accusing and flat.

'So you are. I've got used to your being here, you know. Almost forgot you were only visiting. Take Saturday afternoon off and have a drive around with me. Let's look at some of the old familiar places: Smugglers' Tunnel, Mrs Sharpe's derelict garden, the Lobster Pot.'

'Oh, yes, I'd love that!' All the tension lifted and she was able to smile gratefully at him, relieved at being able to drop the wearisome burden of

Graham's enmity and the knowledge that before Sunday she must make the decision that would definitely change her life.

'Thanks Pete . . . ' She wanted to say more, to let the words flood out, sharing her problems with him as she had done in childhood. But he gave her no chance. Rising quickly, he looked down with eyes that suddenly seemed steely and uncaring. 'Go and have your dinner. I'll pick you up about three on Saturday. OK?'

Without waiting for an answer, he swung away from the bar and left. Gill sighed. Life was very difficult, and so were most people. She had thought that Pete was different, on her side, protective and helpful. Now she wasn't so sure.

She met Lindsey at last on Saturday morning when a young, rather timid voice said her name from the porch of The Lookout as she came down the stairs with some tattered net curtains in her arms.

'Yes, I'm Gill Wayland.' Looking at the short, plump, frizzy-haired girl in jeans and a bright blue anorak, she knew at once who this must be.

'You're Pete's Lindsey . . . ' The words tumbled out, then she bit her lip. What a ridiculous title to give anyone.

But Lindsey's face was colouring prettily, so obviously the relationship was established. 'I'm sorry I couldn't come before. I had the chance of staying for a cookery demonstration by a visiting French chef — I do hope Pete explained?'

'Of course. And I'm glad you're here now.' Gill led the way into the drawing-room, putting her head around the kitchen door as she passed and asking Mrs Campion if they might have some coffee.

Tight lips and an accusing stare warned her of trouble in the offing, but Gill took no notice. She and Mrs Campion had been at loggerheads ever since the day of Uncle Harry's funeral. Now she and Lindsey sat down, smiling warily at each other.

'Pete mentioned that you were looking for a place to live. I shall have a spare room, once I've moved in. I'll be glad to have you, if you like the idea?'

Happily, they discussed rent and the full extent of Lindsey's tenancy. No difficulties presented themselves and by the time a glowering Mrs Campion had presented two mugs of coffee on the table between them, Gill felt she had taken the right step.

'Tell me about your course. I was at the Tech, myself, once.' Just in time, she avoided mentioning Pete's name and, instead, found the new relationship strengthening, as familiar tutors were mentioned.

'Heavens, is old Mr Jarvis still around?'

'He's certainly a bit ancient.' Lindsey smiled, looking so young and pretty that Gill winced.

'Which doesn't say much for my age either; actually, I'm twenty-nine. How old are you, Lindsey?'

'I'll be eighteen next month . . . '

Gill's immediate silent reaction was to condemn Pete for baby-snatching, but she kept control of her tongue, and said aloud, 'Maybe you'd like a party here, at The Lookout? Plenty of room, and I could help with the cooking — '

'That'd be great! Thanks, Gill.'

When Lindsey left they were already well on the way to becoming friends, despite the age difference. A strange situation, Gill thought, as she turned from the front door, after seeing the girl off. But Mrs Campion was standing behind her, and at once Lindsey was forgotten.

'I've had enough,' Mrs Campion grated. 'Ordering me about like that! I'm not staying here any longer. You can find someone else to kowtow to your high 'n mighty London airs — here's my key. And I'd like my money. Right up to this moment, if you please — '

Gill looked at the bothered, embittered woman and felt an unexpected surge of compassion.

'I'm sorry you thought I was giving orders. I hoped I was just asking. But I agree that it might be better if you leave. I can see we'll never get along together, and anyway, I plan to move into the house and run it myself. If you wait a second, I'll get my cheque-book and pay you.'

Cheque tucked into her handbag, winter coat pulled haphazard over her forgotten apron, and a scarf tightly tied around her thin face. Mrs Campion departed. But not without a parting, malicious shot.

'You should take care what you're doing. The whole village is talking about you, you know — and Pete Oakridge seeing you every night at the hotel — and now that little Angus girl coming here. My word, the poor old Lookout's becoming quite a love-nest, isn't it?'

Gill refused to let the degrading

suggestion hurt her. Mrs Campion was angry and only too well did Gill recall the rapid growth and exaggeration of local gossip. Firmly, she told herself that it was all just a storm in a teacup, to be blown out as soon as someone else's name took the fancy of the scandalmongers.

But, as Pete's noisy old car squeaked to a halt outside in the street at five to three, she couldn't help wondering who was watching, and enlarging the already existing rumours. However, Pete gave her little time for such worries.

'Right, I'll show you Graham's house first, then we'll drive up the coast road and have tea at the Grange, then back along the creek. I've booked dinner at the Lobster Pot, so between tea and then we've got to walk ourselves hungry again. What are your shoes like, city lady?'

'Flat and comfy. And I'm no lady!' She threw the comment in with a grin, as she slid into the passenger seat.

Pete looked sideways as he helped to

fasten her seat-belt.

'You're learning,' he said drily, and from then on Gill relaxed as familiar scenes flashed past her window.

'Don't go so fast, Pete — I can't see properly.' She craned her neck, staring back at the old school to which she, Graham and Pete had all gone. Then the car climbed out of the village and up, up, until, looking down, Gill saw the tideline curving the length of the long, scalloped beach, the view almost panoramic as the car chugged wheezily to the crest of the hill.

It stopped halfway along a broad thoroughfare where expensive-looking houses stood in well-manicured lawns and trim gardens.

'Marine Drive? Which is Graham's, then?'

'Can't you guess? The one with the pool, of course.'

'But he always hated swimming!'

'Don't be silly, this is just for show. I don't suppose he's even put his big toe in . . . '

Laughing companionably, they stared with critical eyes at the huge, modernistic block of plate glass, imported stone and strangely angled roof. Gill was awed. 'It must've cost him a bomb. Where on earth did all the money come from? Graham was never a saver.'

'I imagine he has fingers in many pies. A commission here, a golden handshake there . . . ' Pete's voice was suddenly harsh, and Gill stared round at him, surprised. But she said nothing. By now she was aware that Pete had many things on his mind beside the job at the boatyard. She refused to spoil what promised to be a happy afternoon by asking questions, or demanding answers. So she smiled back at him, veiling the curiosity in her eyes, and said lightly, 'C'mon, where do we go next?'

★ ★ ★

As the tide changed, so the cold wind veered around, and a pale sun filtered through the racing clouds. Gill was determined to enjoy the outing, and so she did. They visited echoing, shadowy Smugglers' Tunnel, Mrs Sharple's neglected garden with its flapping and whispering palm-trees, and finally shared a rich cream tea in the discreet silence of The Grange's Victorian drawing-room, in celebration of those childish anniversaries when a visit to the big, rambling house was always a huge treat.

'Help! I'm ready for that walk now ... ' Gill had forgotten just what clotted cream was like; gorgeous but rich.

When Pete parked the car off the road at the head of little Heathway Creek, halfway down the meandering estuary, she was glad of her flat shoes and thick, serviceable duffel coat. The footpath they followed led through muddy meadows and creaking copses of leafless oaks and alders. Her face glowed with health and pleasure as they walked.

'Look, a heron!'

'Remember how you climbed up to a nest in the heronry once — and fell, halfway up?'

'And, thank goodness, you caught me. Oh, Pete, it seems so long ago . . .'

He linked his arm in hers and enjoyment spread through every inch of her body. It was all going so well; she and Pete somehow were as close as they used to be, yet in a new, more mature way. Maybe she'd been wrong about him and Lindsey — maybe?

'I don't know about you, but I'm ready to go back. It's getting dark. And we've got a half-hour drive to the Lobster Pot.' He wheeled her round and dutifully she obeyed.

'I shan't be able to eat a thing.'

'Of course you will. By the time we get there the cream will have sunk without trace, leaving plenty of room for the lobster that I've ordered.'

'Oh, Pete!' She giggled. 'I'm not used to all these hearty rural activities and appetites — oh, help!' She waded into an invisible patch of mud, and nearly fell.

'I've got you — '

His hands were strong and warm, and he pulled her out of the puddle so hard that she nearly collapsed on his chest. The unexpected nearness kept them silent for a long moment. Pete's eyes stared into hers, and Gill's heart began to race.

He murmured in her ear. 'I'm glad you've come back, love.'

Gill shook her head foolishly, not knowing how to reply, not even sure exactly what the casual words intimated. Then he let her go, his voice abruptly nonchalant as ever, and she understood the moment was over.

'Come on, I'll race you the rest of the way back — ' He gave her a start and they both laughed as, neck and neck, they reached the road and the almost-hidden car. Then Pete stopped, his eyes staring intently at the point where deep scrub and willow-bushes masked the entry into the creek from the river beyond. 'It's here again.'

Gill followed his gaze. 'A boat? Whose is it?'

Pete walked towards the car. 'Not sure. It's been here a few times recently. Sneaks in under cover of mist or darkness without the harbour-master or the pilot knowing.'

'How mysterious! Haven't you any idea who owns it?' Gill's question was cut short by the noise of an approaching vehicle. Only just in time did she jump out of the way as a low-slung sports car growled around the corner and stopped some twenty yards farther along, skidding onto the grassy verge and then noisily manoeuvring itself until it was parked beside the shadowy willow-trees, as well hidden as the boat alongside.

Gill stepped near to Pete and saw his eyes narrow in the growing darkness. 'I thought I recognized the man in the passenger seat. But not the driver,' she whispered.

'Quiet — ' he was listening to the voices that wafted through the cold air. Gill heard an inaudible conversation, one voice harsh, with a foreign accent, and the other very familiar.

She pulled at Pete's jacket. 'It was Graham! I'm sure it was!'

But Pete had abruptly lost interest. He looked over his shoulder and grinned sardonically at her. 'There you go again, making things up, as usual! Of course, it wasn't Graham — on a Saturday night, out here in the cold? Don't be daft! He'll be partying in Torquay by now, wining and dining some rich and luscious woman, if I know Graham! In you get, Gill — I don't want to keep that lobster waiting . . . '

He drove off without so much as another glance at either boat or car, and Gill's amazement grew. She was so sure she'd recognized both Graham's face and his voice; and Pete had been as interested as she was, at first. So why this sudden change of attitude?

It was too quick and contrived to be real . . .

Jolting back along the estuary road to Shelmouth, she decided darkly that more mysterious things were happening in this sleepy little village, with its widespread net of intrigue and rumour, than she could possibly have imagined, back in noisy, dirty London.

3

Directly after breakfast on Sunday, Gill telephoned Graham, her voice brisk and to the point.

'Graham? I've phoned to give you my answer about working at the boatyard.'

He sounded vague, and she remembered Pete's hints about late-night revelry on Saturdays. 'What? Is that you, Gill? What a time to ring — you got me out of bed . . . '

She glanced at her watch, saying drily, 'Sorry, but I've got a train to catch to London. And it is nearly *noon*. I'll be down for good in a fortnight, Graham — that's if all goes well. I mean, once the repairs to The Lookout are done, and after I've sold my flat and worked out my two weeks' notice.'

There was a pause. Then Graham's

moody voice barked. 'Don't hurry. I've managed without you for the last few years, after all.'

It was in Gill's mind to say, 'And just look at the state the business is in,' but she bit her tongue, merely repeating that she'd be returning to Shelmouth in fourteen days' time, before ringing off.

The afternoon train returned her to a London engulfed in thick, bitter fog. Fellow travellers' tempers on the tube and bus ran short, and she was thankful to get back to the warmth and privacy of her flat.

After an early supper, she wandered around the rooms, making a mental inventory of all that must be done.

But in bed, uncomfortably sleepless, she lay there, abruptly aghast at the reality of her plans. Leave her snug little home for a vast, old-fashioned, draughty family house? And, even less imaginable at that precise moment, pack-in her high-powered, prestigious job to go and work at the boatyard, with cousin Graham for ever trying to undermine her confidence? Surely she must be mad to take such a step?

Her thoughts rambled on uncontrollably. Leaving Fermoy Restaurants would mean a shrinking of her personal life; there would be no more exciting perks of overseas travel, or meeting celebrities, and the stimulating challenge of being involved in top-level company policy.

Gill, staring unseeingly into the darkness of her room, knew, with sudden, brutal clarity, that if she meant to carry on with her plan of moving back to Shelmouth, she would have to be very determined indeed when facing Roy Aylett, her boss, as she tendered her resignation on Monday morning.

When the moment came, it was even harder than she had feared. Roy Aylett scowled at her from his great height.

'I don't believe a word of all this rigmarole! Of course you can't leave me. You're far too good at your job to go and fritter away all your talents in some silly little seaside business!'

Numbly, she watched as his long, good-looking face registered his thoughts. Anger, dismay, and then — oh, how well she knew him — a thoughtful change of mood, eventually producing the famous, irresistible Aylett charm.

He came over to her chair from the window, below which the West End traffic streamed and hooted, and put an elegant hand on her shoulder.

'My dear Gill, you've had your little joke. Let's just say there'll be a decent rise of salary and another typist to help out, and then we can forget the entire matter. Now — about your proposed visit to Hong Kong to organize the new branch we plan to set up there . . . '

Yes, it had been difficult to convince him that her letter of resignation was all that mattered, but somehow she had done so. But Roy Aylett's last words were to echo in her mind for many months to come before finally she exorcized the memory of them.

'You're heading for disaster, my girl. And unhappiness, I shouldn't wonder.

To be frank, Gill, I think you're a fool.'

★ ★ ★

That night, Gill forced herself to sit quietly by the flickering fire, ignoring the vast amount of work that should, by rights, be tackled now if the move was to take place in a fortnight. Slowly, she faced the undeniable fact that confronted her and which, until now, she had chosen to disregard.

Her real reason for returning to Shelmouth was this urgent and uncomfortable, almost shaming need to be near Pete Oakridge.

For a long time she held the thought in her head, knowing herself to be a naïve, emotional fool. Roy was right, of course — he always was. A disaster, he'd said. And unhappiness?

Gill sighed, then got to her feet as the little French clock on the mantelpiece chimed midnight. Right or wrong, she was hitching her star to a romantic hope that must surely die a death, because it was plain that Pete loved someone else.

Before she got into bed she paused, looking down at the photo of Jeff, still in its usual place on her bedside table. She hadn't looked at it lately, not really looked. Now she did, and knew, feeling half-relieved, half-guilty, that time had already smudged the painful memory of their past loving relationship. The time had come to pick up new threads of life, to step out and meet whatever challenge awaited her.

She loved Pete. In this terrible moment of truth she could admit it at last. But, loving him, she was only too well aware that he was a man with a chip on his shoulder, someone who locked away his feelings, his hopes, and his fears. A difficult man.

But, perhaps as compensation for facing the obstacles, ahead so bravely, Gill slept well and, for once, without troubled dreams. Her last waking thought was that she was finally on course for what must surely be the greatest challenge of her life.

* * *

Two weeks later, with all plans proceeding well, it was Ian Robinson's cheery face that grinned at her as she alighted from the train at Shelmouth Station.

'Hello there, I'm the welcome-home committee!'

Feeling a little weak, Gill just managed to smile back at him. She had been so sure that Pete would be there to meet her. Of course, she hadn't let him know the day and time of her arrival, guessing shrewdly that the village grapevine would inform him.

So her disappointment at not seeing his tall, rangy figure, of being able to bask in his expected smile of warm greeting, was greater than she could have imagined. Now she was grateful for Ian's non-stop chatter which required no answer.

'Mrs Winters — your aunt — asked me to come and meet you. Here, let's have that case — the car's just outside. Terrible weather we've had lately, all gales and wild seas. Today's OK, though — just right for your move, eh? The furniture van got here after dinner, and I took Mrs Winters down to The Lookout about three to see if everything was in place.'

'And was it?' Gill got into the car, bemused by the obvious publicity of her arrival.

'You bet! Looks great it does. Old Tom Harris, the builder, finished the last job yesterday, no problems there. Reckon you'll be as snug as anything with all that double-glazing and roof insulation.'

Ian was still throwing information over his shoulder as he drove out of the station yard. 'And you haven't got to bother about cooking tonight — Pete's blonde, Lindsey, is getting you a meal.'

Gill wasn't sure whether to enthuse at Lindsey's thoughtfulness or to take

Ian to task for linking the girl's name with Pete's.

'She's OK, that Lindsey. Everyone likes her. Friendly. Pretty, too.'

The old insecurity, so firmly denied over the last few weeks, abruptly attacked Gill again. Life was certainly hitting her below the belt; here she was, only five minutes into her new environment, and already Lindsey was made to sound like a rival. And, to make matters worse, a competent and popular rival.

Lindsey's warm welcome didn't help. Gill almost wished she could find some reason for complaint as she enthusiastically conducted her over the newly-repaired and decorated house. But everything looked beautiful, and Gill's furniture and possessions appeared to fit in as though they had been made for the comfortable proportions of The Lookout.

'I've got a meal on, Gill — I didn't want you to have to fuss about in the kitchen on your first night here. You must have had such a hectic time lately, getting ready to move.'

It was with a feeling of resigned relief that Gill sat down to share the supper Lindsey produced a little later.

Pigeon casserole and a bottle of red wine did much to soothe her harassed state of mind, and halfway through the excellent lemon-meringue pie that followed, Gill was able to smile more freely at the face opposite her, knowing that, in all honesty, she must accept this gesture of proffered friendship and concern.

'What a smashing meal,' she said warmly. 'I do appreciate the kind thought and all the hard work, Lindsey. You really are a super cook.'

Lindsey's smile was reward enough. 'I was glad to do it. It's so marvellous knowing I've got a new home here. I can't thank you enough for letting me come, Gill. Things have got a bit awkward at home, one way and another.'

Her face clouded sadly, and Gill

resisted the urge to ask why. She guessed that Lindsey would eventually confide in her as their friendship developed, and then pushed the thought away. Such a confidence must necessarily include mention of Pete, and Gill knew she wasn't ready to hear any details of their relationship.

But later, in the shared intimacy of the quiet sitting-room, with the old familiar childhood nostalgia crowding in on her thoughts, Gill suddenly longed to ask where Pete was. If only he had turned up this evening, just to say hello.

His whispered words, as he had held her tightly in that never-to-be-forgotten moment at Heathway Creek, rang around her weary head. 'I'm glad you've come back, love.' Had he meant them or not?

Looking across the hearth, Gill saw Lindsey watching her and could bear the stress of the memory no longer. Abruptly, she put down her cup and stood up.

'Think I'll have an early night. Thanks again for the meal. See you . . . '

She left the room quickly, not waiting for the soft-voiced reply.

Numbly, as she climbed the crooked staircase, Gill prayed that a good night's sleep would produce a more confident and positive attitude in the morning. Suddenly, it was vital that she should face the new day with fresh vigour and strength.

★ ★ ★

Brilliant light fell directly on to Gill's face as she roused from a refreshing sleep. For a second she wondered where she was. No hum of the London rush-hour traffic, but, instead a raucous chorus of seagulls' cries from the roof above. Her mind raced. Shelmouth. The Lookout. She was actually here, in her new home — and the new job awaited her.

She was out of bed in one quick movement, pulling back the pale-green floral curtains, looking around and catching her breath at the beauty of what she saw.

It was full tide, the grey-green waters of the English Channel filling her vision, swelling and rolling splendidly as they scattered rough handfuls of foam over all that remained of the beach, just a stone's-throw from the house.

Opening wide the window, she smelt the tang of salt, felt the wild wind leap at her face and hair, and knew a moment of joy, even as she shivered. She had been right to come back. Oh, yes, now she knew it.

On the dot of nine o'clock she was unlocking Graham's new office, one of the two rooms he had surlily agreed to rent from her, being part of the old house she had no wish to use. Uncle Harry's office was now unrecognizable, save for the familiar view of the harbour behind, and the long aspect of the boatyard, visible from an interior window.

The ancient swivel-chair, long used by Uncle Harry himself, had been replaced by a modern, tubular-steel monstrosity, and tall filing-cabinets crowded the light-painted walls. A word-processor stood on a second, smaller desk, with all its software clustered importantly around it.

Gill, appraising what she saw, forced herself to forget Uncle Harry's haunting presence, and admitted that the new look of the old room was impressive. An up-to-date office which should be easy to run.

But then she noticed the bulging in-tray on the main desk, the untidy pile of letters, some still in their envelopes, unopened, the heap of advertising matter, catalogues and brochures, that fell across the polished surface. Closing the door behind her, and wondering briefly when Graham would choose to appear, Gill began to try and sort things out.

She had achieved some semblance of order, putting the more important matters on the top of the pile of work to be dealt with, when the door behind her opened. She turned quickly, ready to chastise Graham for being late — childhood memories urging her to attack before he did — but it was a woman who hastily entered, blinking at her in surprise.

'You must be Miss Wayland. I'm Mrs Harvey, Graham's typist. I'm sorry I couldn't get here before, but it's my husband, you see. He's still in intensive care after his heart attack last week, and what with trying to get his washing done and buying a few bits and pieces to take him after work — well, the time just slipped by, I'm afraid.'

Gill smiled compassionately at the harassed face, still showing signs of tears and distress.

'Don't worry, Mrs Harvey. It's good of you to come at all. I'm sorry I didn't know about your husband.'

'You mean Graham didn't tell you?'

'I expect he was going to — but I've not yet seen him.'

Mrs Harvey sighed, absent-mindedly removing her headscarf. 'Always late, Graham is. And there's so much for him to do — I told him last Friday he ought to answer those letters, but he rushed off early in the afternoon.'

Mrs Harvey began unbuttoning her coat but Gill said firmly, 'I suggest you go home again, Mrs Harvey and forget all about the work. I'm here now, and I'll stand in for you until your husband's better and you're not feeling so upset.'

'Well, if you're sure — ' Anxiety lifted and Mrs Harvey's tense face slid into a grateful, moist-eyed smile.

Gill watched her go, then returned to the pile of letters on the desk before her. She was glad to have been able to remove at least one burden from the poor, harassed woman, and glad, too, of the chance of working on her own, trying to organize Graham's chaotic and inefficiently abandoned workload.

The junior from the reception office in the yard brought in coffee at ten forty-five, but there was still no sign of Graham.

What a way to run a business, Gill muttered to herself as once more she settled down to work. No wonder the boatyard was in such a state of neglect and uneasiness if the managing director didn't keep a firm hand on its helm.

Suddenly she heard a voice calling Pete's name over the tannoy.

'Mr Oakridge, will you go to the slipway, please.'

To her annoyance, Gill felt her heart beating faster. Frowning, she tried to keep concentrating on her work, but it was no good. Pete's image came between her and the letters on the desk. She couldn't resist crossing the office to the window that looked down into the well of the yard.

At first she saw only gangs of occupied men, cutting timber, welding metal and working on the half-finished boat keels that filled the long, roofed yard. And there was Graham's pride and joy, the newly-built, innovative, motor cruiser, *Melinda II*, moored alongside the slip, undergoing last-minute refitting.

From the pile of correspondence on Graham's desk, Gill had learned that Monsieur Phillipe Leconte was buying the boat at what seemed to her to be an exorbitant price. She hoped, a little anxiously, that Graham's trendy ideas and refinements would be worth such a large sum of money and, indeed, further the reputation of Wayland's Boatyard.

She wondered how *Melinda* had fared in sea trials. No doubt Graham had made important improvements since the prototype, *Melinda I*, went down last year, causing Jack Oakridge's death.

The thought immediately returned Pete to her mind, and then she saw him, coming out of his own small hutted office, heading for the slipway. He passed directly beneath the window where she stood, and unexpectedly glanced up, as if trying to see if she was already installed in the office, but Gill dodged out of sight.

At once, she berated herself. Why on earth couldn't she have smiled down at him and waved, letting him know she was here as planned? Her sense of personal dismay was heightened as she watched him reach the gangway where *Melinda II* was moored.

The craft looked sleek and seaworthy, her pale-blue hull and chrome fittings shining in the morning light. She rode the full tide with confidence, rocking in a smooth, controlled lilt, as the water lapped gently at her sides.

Gill saw Pete come to a halt beside the girl in the scarlet anorak and matching trousers who stood by the boat. She saw how Brigitte Leconte's welcoming, vivacious smile brought an answering grin to Pete's sombre face, and soon they were deep in what appeared to be mutually enjoyable conversation.

Bleakly, Gill wondered if her recent gibe at Pete's harem had been a hit in the dark — did he, indeed, deal in numbers of girls, and so keep his bachelordom intact?

She thought back over the years, trying to recall whether the younger Pete had shown earlier signs of such flirtatiousness, and decided, with a feeling of relief, that he'd been single-minded with, as far as she knew, only herself as his adolescent girlfriend. Watching how he and Brigitte continued their talk, with smiles and easy laughter punctuating the words she could only guess at, Gill wondered uneasily if Pete, knowing that Graham considered Brigitte to be his property, was merely trying to separate them by chatting Brigitte up in this way. But if so, why — out of malice, because he and Graham had always been at loggerheads and were especially so now?

After a few more minutes, Gill gave up and turned from the window. She couldn't stand seeing Pete look down at the French girl in that intimate way; the way he had looked at her in Heathway Creek, only a couple of weeks ago.

* * *

She was doggedly battling on with letters and queries, when voices rang in the passage outside, and the door thrust open to reveal Graham, followed closely by Pete himself. It was very obvious that a row was in progress. Both men's voices were raised, and Graham checked in mid-stride as soon as he saw Gill sitting at the secretary's table, without changing the belligerent expression on his face.

'What on earth — Where's Mrs Harvey? What are you doing here, Gill. And what's all *that*?'

He reached her side, flicking a rough hand across the papers, scattering them untidily as he did so.

Looking into his angry face, Gill managed to smile calmly as she shuffled the letters together again. But irritation crept into her voice as she answered sharply, 'Don't be so heavy-handed, Graham — it's taken me a couple of hours to sort out this lot. I sent Mrs Harvey home. She's in no state to do anything but look after her poor husband at the moment. Lucky that I was here, don't you think?'

They stared at each other and the air seemed charged with mutual antipathy. Gill was aware of Pete, in the background, crossing the room and looking out of the window overlooking the harbour. Clearly he had no wish to be involved in their squabble. Despite her annoyance, Gill found herself wondering darkly if he was looking for Brigitte.

She broke the lengthy pause, saying drily, 'I hope you're here to do some work, Graham. I've done what I can, but a lot of these queries are too technical for me to deal with.'

Graham turned away, flinging himself into a sitting attitude on the side of his desk, to stare back at her with a sneering expression.

'You mean you actually don't know enough about boats to cope yourself? Exactly! Just what I meant, when I said you were mad to think you could come here and start lording it — '

'I *can* learn, Graham. And fast.' Gill was on her feet, glad to be able to spill out some of her own anger in reply to his sarcasm.

'I earned my old job at Fermoy's by doing just that — learning fast — so don't make the mistake of thinking I'm only a copy-typist. Of course I can deal with all this, on an executive level, given the right information, and a little more time. *And* some personal backing from you, if that's not asking too much — '

Again, the silence. Graham got up moodily, walking around his desk, one hand smoothing the chrome top of his managerial chair. He looked away from Gill, to where Pete stood by the window, then back at her again. By now his face was showing no anger, and he seemed merely pensive.

Gill wished she knew what he was thinking, but his next words told her very little.

Suddenly he was smiling, his voice breezy as he remarked, 'Well, I suppose I must be thankful I haven't got to bother finding a new typist while old Ma Harvey is away. Had a terrible job finding a temp when she was on holiday — and then the girl who came couldn't spell, and somehow managed to break the word-processor. At least you'll do better than that, won't you, Gilly?'

The wind taken out of her sails, Gill had no ready reply. She watched him turn towards Pete.

'So, *Melinda II*'s all set for delivery? Monsieur Leconte declines to pay the final account until he takes possession. Who's ferrying her across?'

Pete took his hands out of his pockets and met Graham's eyes.

'Not me,' he said quietly, his face deadpan. 'The first *Melinda* killed my dad; I don't reckon on running the same danger, thanks. Neil Peters can take her.'

Graham was furious, his face instantly patched with colour as he snapped back, 'That's a load of nonsense! The new boat's been improved and checked on sea trials. The reports were, excellent. And it's not true that Jack died because of any weakness on *Melinda*'s part — it was an accident, and you know it!'

'Do I?'

'The coroner said so.' Graham's angry impetus had died, and he started blustering in the old familiar way.

Gill wondered curiously why this matter of the accident should still evoke such passionate feelings on both men's parts, if it was, indeed, a safely shut case.

Pete moved from the window and she caught a glimpse of his expression before he reached the door, turning away from her to open it. She snatched in a breath.

There it was again, that glimpse

of fierce and relentless determination lighting up his eyes, setting his jaw into heavy, intractable lines, as if a secret hatred had momentarily surfaced. And then he looked back, smiling casually at Graham, saying over his shoulder, 'OK, let's forget it. I'll tell Neil to organize the trip.

'Oh, and by the way, I think Brigitte will want to go with him. She says she's an experienced crew member, and I doubt if Neil will mind having her aboard . . . ' His smile deepened, the insinuation clear.

Graham slammed his chair with a heavy fist, looking thunderous. 'No question of her going. I wouldn't trust Peters, and anyway, it's too dangerous, a girl like that taking part in the maiden voyage — '

Pete had the last word. 'But I understood you to say that *Melinda II* is far safer than her prototype?' he said innocently. 'Oh, well, just as you like, Graham. I'll tell her your decision.'

The door closed, and Gill watched Graham's scowl slowly die. Then, unexpectedly, the door reopened and Pete smiled warmly into her disbelieving eyes.

'Forgive me, love,' he said disarmingly. 'What with one thing and another, I forgot my manners. Great to see you here, Gill. Hope everything works out OK.'

'Thanks, Pete.' Taken aback, she watched him leave the room, her head whirling. Talk about an unknown quantity — Pete Oakridge was certainly that.

Then Graham was at her side, frowning down at the work on the desk.

'Look, I've got an appointment — won't be back till later this afternoon. You can manage here, can't you, Gilly?'

The frown slid into a persuasive smile, and his voice was falsely jolly. 'Good old Gill! You know, I think we might get on quite well, after all.

See you later, eh? Cheers for now, then . . .'

He left the room in a hurry, and she heard him yelling down the yard, telling someone to ask Mademoiselle Leconte to wait, he'd be with her in just a couple of minutes.

Fascinated, Gill again took up her position at the interior window. After a brief pause, she saw Brigitte saunter down from the slipway and walk towards Pete's office, where she propped herself against the doorway, chatting to Pete, who sat inside.

When Graham, marched into the yard, minutes later, she moved quickly, taking his arm and flashing her wide-eyed smile at him with obvious enjoyment. They went off together, with Graham being unusually attentive and seemingly agreeable. Gill's mouth twitched as she watched the drama.

And then, just as she was about turn from the window, a movement in the doorway of Pete's office made her continue to watch. She saw him come outside, watching Graham and Brigitte as they left the yard. When they'd disappeared from view, he still stood there, and Gill's heart beat faster as she perceived the stony look on his thoughtful, darkly-shadowed face.

She had never known jealousy before, but she did so then, to her own consternation. It hurt deeply, to see Pete watching Brigitte — in fact, it was all Gill could do to restrain herself from running down into the yard and claiming his attention for herself.

But then the telephone rang and conditioned as she was to putting business before personal matters, she turned to answer it.

'Good-morning. Wayland's Boatyard — may I help you?'

'Where is Graham, please? I wish to speak to him — '

Gill's interest flared. The voice was heavy, and slightly difficult to understand because of the foreign accent. Hadn't she heard it before somewhere? Infuriatingly, the occasion eluded her, but she was certain the voice was familiar.

Intrigued, she played for time. 'Perhaps you'd like to leave a message, Mr — er — er . . . '

There was a pause, and she frowned, willing the caller not to hang up. Then the thickly-accented voice said hesitantly, 'No, no, I wish to speak only to Graham. He will be back later, yes? I will telephone again.'

Very quickly, Gill chipped in, 'I'm sorry, but I'm afraid that's no good. Mr Wayland has an appointment that will keep him busy until after office hours.'

Despite her anxiety, she smiled briefly, imagining Graham prolonging his 'appointment' with Brigitte well into the evening. 'And I'm sure he'd be upset at not getting your message, so perhaps you could tell me what it's about?'

She held her breath and then released it, slow and silent, as the man on the other end of the wire said doubtfully,

'Well — but no, I don't think — '

Inspiration hit Gill. She crossed her fingers as the white lie came to her, feeling a quick surge of urgency. She *must* find out what Graham was up to . . .

Firmly, and with all the relaxed confidence her employment with Fermoy's had given her, Gill said, 'I haven't made myself very clear, I'm afraid. Actually, I am Mr Wayland's partner — we work together, you see, and so I'm used to sharing all his business projects and matters. I can assure you that any message will be treated in the strictest confidence — '

Another pause. And then, just as she was certain the caller was too doubtful to say any more, she heard the office door swing open, and Pete came in.

Swiftly, she looked over her shoulder, mouthing to him to stay, and then smiling with relief as the foreign voice sounded once again in her ear.

'Very well, I leave you my message. Tell Graham that the next trip must be delayed until Thursday. Too difficult for Erik to come on Tuesday, you say. He will understand.'

'Right. Yes, I've got it down, and I'll make sure he gets the message as soon as possible, Mr — er — Erik, was it? Sorry, but I didn't get your full name —'

'No name. Goodbye.'

* * *

As the dialling tone sounded, Gill reluctantly replaced the receiver. She scribbled the caller's exact words on a pad and then turned to smile at Pete, standing in the open doorway.

'It was him!' she said excitedly. 'The man who was with Graham that night at Heathway Creek —'

Pete frowned. 'Calm down, Gill. You only thought you recognized Graham. And as for the other chap, well, faces, all look alike in the shadows, you know.'

Dismay made her voice sharp. 'Don't

be ridiculous — I *know* it was Graham. And I know it was the same foreign voice I heard — this man who just phoned was definitely the man he was with. I mean — well, listen to the message he left. If this doesn't tally up with that mysterious boat and Graham being there incognito, I don't know what else will.'

She bent to pick up the pad, but Pete forestalled her, moving so fast that she stood, staring, as it was flicked out of her hand.

She saw his face harden as he stared down at what she had written. Then he threw the pad down onto the desk, giving her a look so furious and unfamiliar that she felt herself quail.

'For heaven's sake! What's all this double-Dutch? I can't read a word of it — '

'Of course you can't.' Her voice was as cold and withdrawn as his. She didn't like the stranger that stood in Pete's shoes. 'It's shorthand. I'll read you what it says.'

Her hand had begun to tremble, but she forced herself to remain calm. Slowly and clearly she read the message.

Looking up, she met Pete's eyes and saw within them a surge of the same excitement that had first fired her when the caller rang. And then, even as she began to smile again, and saw a similar response thaw Pete's set face, Graham's voice reached her from the open doorway.

'Get out, you two damned busybodies! Taking my phone calls, taking over my office . . . good God, I don't want any more of it!'

Like a whirlwind, he came in, snatching the pad from Gill's hand and tearing off the sheet bearing the message. Then he crumpled it fiercely, before throwing it wildly into the waste-bin at the side of the room.

His whole body was shaking uncontrollably, his face rigid with fury, and instinctively Gill stepped backwards, almost wincing as he continued to yell, his voice rising higher and getting even louder as the words tumbled out.

'Get out, Gill — and you, Pete — before I really lose my temper . . . '

4

Gill was shocked into silence by Graham's explosive outburst. She had always known him to be quick-tempered, but now he seemed to be poised on the threshold of violence. His tirade of frantic words fell about her, and she could only wait for his rage to exhaust itself.

Pete came across to put his arm around her shoulders and said coldly, 'Shut it, Graham. No need to be rude simply because Gill took a phone call for you. One of the reasons she's here is surely to share the work and help out . . . '

But Graham hadn't finished. His face contorted with anger as he spat out even more words of hate and contempt at the two of them.

'Oh, trust you to be on her side, Pete. Always were, weren't you? The two of you scheming against me — and Dad, too. The story of my life! Well, things have changed now, and *I'm* in control. So you needn't think you and Gill can get away with it any longer — '

Pete turned his back contemptuously. 'For God's sake, Graham, grow up!'

But Graham was in full flood, clearly unable to stop himself. His plump face was wreathed in a malevolent smile that made Gill shudder.

'Grow up? But isn't that just what we've all done? And especially you, Pete . . . don't suppose I don't know what you've got in your rotten, grown-up mind these days! You worked on Dad till he was so moithered he actually thought you a better son than *me*! And now you're planning to do the same with our local heiress . . . '

Gill's mouth fell open. What was he on about? Had he gone out of his mind? But she had no opportunity of interrupting, for Graham was still blathering on.

'Yes, you've got it all worked out, I bet. Marry Gill and get hold of her shares in the business. Well, even if you do' — Graham doubled his fist and shook it wildly in Pete's direction — 'you won't get your filthy hands on my boatyard!

'Even with half the shares between you, I'll still get the majority vote . . . because the men in the yard know I'm the old man's son, and you're only a village idiot who's wormed his way up . . . '

Something in Gill found it imperative to stop this inane drivel that made Graham resemble the scheming child he had always been. His ranting was distasteful and embarrassing.

Even without Pete's protective arm enfolding her any longer, she was strong enough to say sharply, 'That'll do, for heaven's sake! You're making an exhibition of yourself. Look, Graham, calm down and let's get back to business. These letters, now . . . '

'Blast the letters.' Still he glowered,

but looked less violent. 'We'll deal with them later. But that phone call — '

Abruptly, Gill had an instinctive feeling that this could be the moment to solve the mystery of the foreign caller. Graham was still so plainly off-keel from his outburst that maybe he would give a true answer, without trying to cover up as he would doubtless do in a more controlled mood.

She chose her words with care.

'This Erik, who phoned — he wouldn't give another name. And the delayed delivery. I hope I got it right, Graham? Does it make sense? Do you understand . . . '

But in the middle of the sentence, she found Pete back at her side, turning to face her, frowning and shaking his head.

She bit off her last words, dismayed. She had been about to go on and ask Graham openly about the night, a fortnight ago, when she had been so sure he was the visitor to the boat hidden at Heathway Creek.

But there was that forbidding expression on Pete's face again, the steel in his blue eye daring her to say any more. And then, even as he turned back to Graham, she watched, confused, how his expression swiftly changed. Once again, he was the old friendly, rather ironic Pete of their childhood.

'Look, Graham, I'm sorry about all this. We've probably both said a lot of nonsensical things that we'd rather forget. Well, I will if you will; how about it then?'

Graham muttered something inaudible, and looked almost ashamed of himself. Watching, Gill could hardly believe how Pete had so deftly handled a highly explosive situation. And she was even more surprised when, leaning on the desk and grinning down at Graham's averted face, Pete added nonchalantly, 'To change the subject — what have you been up to with Brigitte Leconte, you old womanizer?

'Did you manage to persuade her not

to make the voyage on *Melinda II*? I wouldn't put anything past you — you always had a honeyed tongue when it was worth your while . . . '

Graham rose to the bait instantly. The last traces of his anger died completely, and he smiled, a sly expression of pride making his eyes gleam.

'That's it!' he said bouncily. 'A word from me, and she changed her mind! I'm going to take her over to France on the ferry and then we'll drive south together. Spend a couple of days in Cannes — how about that, then?'

Pete stood upright, still smiling. 'Nice going,' he said quietly, and Gill flinched as she realized with dismay that all Pete's previous friendliness had been merely pretence. He hated Graham with an intensity that scared her.

Clearly, he planned to get the best of him, for some as yet unknown reason. Deep inside her, Gill felt a tremble of fear, and wanted to run.

But Graham was talking again, as if

nothing unpleasant had happened between them. He was smiling, toying with the gold pen that rested incongruously on Uncle Harry's Victorian inkwell, leaning back in the monstrous, modern chair, and clearly enjoying himself.

'Before we go, why don't we have a party! Brigitte and I, and anyone you care to ask, Pete . . . oh, and Gilly, of course. Up at my place.'

Gill watched him appear to swell with pride as he continued, 'Haven't seen it, have you, eh? Some house! I might tell you that the plot of land alone cost ten thousand. And it's increasing all the time — let's make it next Tuesday. That OK with you?'

Without waiting for an answer, he dropped the pen and got to his feet.

Gill watched him swagger to the door, her mind churning. His behaviour just didn't make sense. First, that appalling rage; then the wild outburst of fantastic suspicions. And now of all things, a friendly invitation to dinner! What on earth was wrong with Graham?

In the doorway, he turned back to beam at them both. 'I'll go and tell Brigitte,' he said happily. 'She loves a party. And it'll take her mind off wanting to go on the *Melinda* with Peters . . .'

The door slammed behind him, and Gill let out her breath slowly, looking across the office at Pete, hardly knowing what to expect next. But he was leaning against the window-frame, seemingly unbothered and at ease.

He shot her a smile that revealed nothing. 'Good old Graham,' he said mildly. 'Always comes up trumps in the end. You'll find his house — well, interesting . . . and very valuable.'

The twinkle in his blue eyes was irresistible, and Gill found herself laughing as she sank down into the chair behind her own desk, relief chasing away the tension of the last few minutes.

'I'm sure I shall! But, Pete . . .'

Suddenly she needed to be frank with him, wanting to discuss Graham's extraordinary behaviour, to make guesses about the strange phone call — but he was already on his way to the door, and the smile was gone.

'Better get back to work,' he said abruptly, and left.

Gill felt as if she had been at the receiving end of a hurricane. Her nerves were frayed and her mind couldn't stop reliving the unpleasant scene. But she applied herself to the work, and slowly began to relax.

The afternoon wore on, and soon after the junior had come in with her mug of tea, she had to put on the light. A quick look at the harbour showed menacing storm clouds racketing up from the south-west, and even with double-glazing Gill thought she could hear the windows rattling in their frames as the wind increased in strength and noise.

When the yard siren sounded at five o'clock, she stretched her stiff body, and, with relief, put away the pile of letters and queries that still needed attention.

As she locked the office door on leaving, she felt a return of slight apprehension. Supposing Graham came back — supposing he walked into The Lookout and made another scene . . . the idea made her recoil, and she had to tell herself very strong-mindedly that she was in her own home, and that Graham had no right of entry into it without her knowledge and permission.

Thank goodness she had decided on fitting a double-locking device on the connecting door between her own quarters and the two rented office rooms.

★ ★ ★

As she entered The Lookout, it seemed very dark and very empty. Lindsey wasn't yet back from college, and Gill found it unexpectedly difficult to settle down in the new drawing-room, despite its familiar furniture and newly-established elegance.

Although it was only early evening, she succumbed to the persuasion of having a drink to cheer herself up, and sat down by the crackling fire with a glass of sherry. But, no doubt about it, she still felt upset.

Impossible to ignore Graham's outburst, to forget his suggestion that Pete wanted to marry her for her share of the business — and, most of all, impossible to forget the look on Pete's set face, the chill, icy chips in his deep eyes.

Doubts came and went, only to return again, magnified. Dismay grew as first Graham's face, and then Pete's, flickered through her racing mind, and so her first evening in her new home — in her new life — was spent in an unhappy mishmash of fears and foreboding.

But Gill was no coward. And by the next morning she had decided, sensibly, to put everything behind her. She would accept Graham's invitation to dinner — why not? It would at least be a laugh, inspecting his trendy abode. And she would invite Pete to go with her! She'd ask him today — before he had a chance, maybe, to invite Lindsey instead of her.

★ ★ ★

As she unlocked the office door at nine o'clock, Gill mentally squared her shoulders and lifted her head a degree higher. She must do her best to fight this peculiar, secret war that appeared to be going on between Graham and Pete. She must get on with her own life and leave them to theirs.

And so an acceptable pattern slowly fell around her. Gill found the office work increasingly interesting and sufficiently challenging to satisfy her high standards of efficiency and intelligence.

Occasionally, she made trips into the

boatyard itself in search of facts not always available from catalogues and brochures, or the terse notes Graham left in answer to her queries.

Fred Hooker's son, Derek, was in charge of stores, and shared his father's native garrulity. He always produced a smile and instant attention when Gill entered the long, crowded little building, with the polished counter running the length of it.

After a couple of such visits, Derek's smile grew even more welcoming, and he leaned towards her very confidentially as she prepared to return to her own office, a sheaf of catalogues in her hand.

'Heard the latest, Miss? That French girl, Brigitte somebody, has got Graham eating out of her hand . . . good for him, eh?'

Gill bit her lip. It was bad form and extremely foolish to gossip with staff. But she dearly wanted to know more details, hoping to learn possible facts pointing to the reason for Graham's strange behaviour patterns.

She compromised, merely saying mildly. 'Well, well. How did you hear that, Derek?'

He winked, leaning on the counter.

'When a girl's as attractive as that one, Miss, she's hot news! All the gossips have got their eyes on her, you can bet. They don't miss a trick, that lot. And so the word gets round, see?'

Gill stepped away, momentarily chilled. 'I suppose it does.' Her smile cracked and, hastily, she made for the door. 'Thanks for your help, Derek.'

She felt him watching her as she made her way through the yard, and she was abruptly and hatefully aware of how all the other eyes must be focused on her, although, none were as brazen as Derek's. For if Brigitte was 'hot news', then so was she . . . Graham's cousin, vying with him for a position in the family business.

Was every man in the yard secretly watching her, perhaps even laying bets on how the struggle would work out?

Did their wives smirk and disapprove as the gossip was brought home? A terrible thought brought her to an abrupt stop — even believing what Graham had shouted, that Pete was trying to court her in order to get her shares? Oh, God, surely not! Was her every move watched and commented on by the invisible band of scandalmongers?

The idea brought the blood surging into her throat and face. She stumbled on through the yard, unable to look at any of the boys and men who worked in little groups all around her.

Back in the office, she sat down, staring sightlessly at the far wall. She wished, with all her heart, that she had never come back. That she was still in London, perhaps, anywhere, but not in Shelmouth, and the focus of everyone's fantasies in Wayland's Boatyard.

In the afternoon, Aunt Mary arrived, ushered into the office by a smiling Anna with an offer of some tea. Gill made her very welcome, settling her into Graham's huge chair with her back to the window.

'Lovely to see you, Aunt Mary. I planned to come to see you at the weekend, but you've beaten me to it. You look very smart — is that a new hat?'

Aunt Mary's careworn face lightened slightly. 'Yes, dear. I didn't think poor Harry would mind me not wearing black any longer.' She leaned forward, and her smile faded. 'Gill, I've come about Graham . . . '

Lightly, a smile forced to her lips, Gill said, 'And what about Graham, Aunt Mary?' Her shoulders tensed. She had seen little of Graham since the recent row, but knew he had visited the office in the evenings, when she wasn't there. Apparently, he preferred to work alone, out of sight of her all-too-critical eyes.

'Well, people have been talking . . . ' Aunt Mary smiled anxiously, and fidgetted with her teacup. 'They do, you know, Gill. This is a small place, and things get around. And Graham is well-known . . . '

Gill sighed. 'All right, tell me the worst. You've heard that Graham and Pete and I had words, I suppose?'

'Yes, dear, that's it.' Aunt Mary looked unaccountably stubborn, and Gill waited for further information. When it was obvious none was coming, she said persuasively, 'So what are you worried about, Aunt Mary? We all made it up. In fact, Graham has asked us up to his house for dinner next week.'

'I'm not really worried, Gill; just afraid that you might be. I mean . . . ' Aunt Mary looked down at her veined hands. 'I'm used to the way they argue. Even fight, sometimes. As boys they were always at it. But they made friends again, afterwards. Now — well, now that you're here, I'm afraid you'll get involved as well. And, of course, you mustn't. You must keep out of it.'

Gill stared. Keep out of what?

Petty sparring between two overgrown schoolboys? 'Oh, come on, Aunt Mary! You're not serious, surely? Of course I'm not involved in anything that goes on between the two of them . . . '

Aunt Mary looked upset, and her mouth quivered as she said unevenly. 'But you *are*, my dear. You and Pete have become — well, special friends, I suppose. He told Mrs Fairweather that he was delighted you'd come home. And Mrs Fairweather said — '

Gill held up a hand. 'Don't tell me,' she said grimly. 'I can imagine only too well! Look, Aunt — this is just village gossip going around. Pete and I are in no way ganging up against poor old Graham.' For a second she thought hard. 'And even if we did — well, would it matter?'

'Of course it would!' Aunt Mary's voice was uncharacteristically sharp, and her eyes widened. 'You mustn't upset Graham, whatever happens, Gill. Promise me you won't upset him . . . '

'But why?' Gill bit her lip as she saw

the anxiety surface on her aunt's lined face. 'All right, you needn't worry, Aunt. I'll pour oil on any troubled water that drifts my way from now on!'

She made her voice light and smiled reassuringly. 'And, if there are any more hard words when we visit Graham's house, I'll be a mediator, you have my word for it. Now cheer up! How about another cup of tea?'

The awkward moment was done with, the subject closed. Aunt Mary eventually returned home, and Gill went on with her work. But the fact that Graham must in no circumstances be upset stayed in her mind for a long time. Why? she asked herself? *Why*?

★ ★ ★

A likely answer came out of the blue next day when, taking a brief stroll along the prom after a snack lunch, Gill bumped into Fred Hooker, who was heading for the shelter by the pier, and was persuaded to exchange greetings with him.

Chatty as ever, Fred dropped hint upon hint about Graham's misdeeds at the boatyard; about his rows with Mr Harry in the old days; about his relationship with Brigitte Leconte; and finally even brought Pete into the one-sided conversation as well.

'Those two, now — always on at each other. 'Tisn't right, never is. But there, man'boy, they was always the same. Pete's a good workman, and a fine sailor. While Graham don't like the sea one little bit . . . '

Fred's hook-nosed face softened as the memories glowed in his mind. 'T'was a good thing as Jack Oakridge, Pete's dad, was on the *Melinda I* last year when Graham were sailing her. For Graham'd just had one of his funny turns, see? Hardly knew what 'e were doing, poor lad. No wonder the boat went out of control.'

Gill let the old man ramble on, too busy thinking her own thoughts to hear

141

the end of the story. When he paused for breath, she smiled, said she must get back to work, and left him in the shelter, looking out to sea with faded eyes. His words filled her head as she returned briskly to The Lookout and the afternoon's work — Graham with one of his funny turns . . .

She wondered just what a 'funny turn' entailed, and decided to ask Pete, whom she hadn't seen since the row the other day.

With a feeling of happy anticipation, she timed her arrival at the yard entrance as Pete left, a little after five o'clock. On her lips was the ready excuse of having an errand to do in the village.

She thought Pete's usually sombre face lit up as soon as he saw her. He certainly sounded friendly.

'Hi! I've been meaning to come to see you, but there's been too much hassle going on in the yard. Everything OK your end, Gill?'

'Fine.'

She fell easily into step with him, and they walked through the village towards Pete's cottage at the far end of the long, deserted beach. Two dogs chased each other over the glistening sands, and a herring-gull sat on the church spire, wailing mournfully. Gill felt at home and relaxed. She chattered without any trouble.

'I've managed to sift through the pile of stuff in the office, and dear Graham comes in at night to oversee things, and leaves me dictatorial notes! It's not a bad working arrangement.

'By the way, Pete' — she turned her head to smile determinedly at him and saw that he was already watching her — 'about having dinner with Graham on Tuesday . . . ' For a second she paused, then took a deep breath. 'Will you take me, please?'

She had expected a quick and amiable acceptance to the question, for the expression on his face was friendly and so, at first, she couldn't believe that he didn't answer her.

'Well — come on! Yes or no?' She hadn't meant her voice to sound so indignant and ungracious. She only wanted to jerk him into action. Of course, if he preferred to ask Lindsey instead of her, then she would have to put up with it. But she needed to know.

'OK, then,' he said at last, still not looking at her.

'Thanks very much,' she said coldly. 'But you don't have to be *quite* so enthusiastic.' The little snap of sarcasm helped to relieve the pain that welled up inside her, but it seemed to needle Pete even further.

Sharply, he turned to look at her. 'I said I'd take you, for heaven's sake. What else do you expect?'

Gill flinched at the severity in his eyes. 'Nothing. Absolutely nothing. I'm sorry . . . ' She watched his eyes deepen, heard a tone of apology enter his low voice, and felt his hand suddenly reaching out to grasp hers, warm and strong, his fingers betraying the depth of his own emotion.

'I'm the one to be sorry, love. All this business with Graham rattles me, I'm afraid. Find I'm shooting my mouth off without thinking . . . forgive me?'

Melting, she knew she could forgive him anything, just as long as he went on looking at her like that and holding her hand. Words seemed unnecessary, and so she merely nodded, smiling her agreement.

At Pete's cottage door, they halted. 'I won't ask you in,' he said lightly, releasing her hand to find his key. 'The maid's day off, I'm afraid . . . '

In the light of the nearby street lamp, they smiled at each other and Gill answered without thinking. 'You scruffy old bachelor! I can just imagine the state the cottage is in! What you need is a woman around the place . . . ' She stopped abruptly, as Pete's smile died. 'I mean . . . ' She floundered, suddenly lost in images of buxom, competent Lindsey, and was unable to finish the sentence, no longer even sure what she did mean.

Was Lindsey in the cottage? Was she the woman in his life? Gill's head reeled, and Pete's inscrutable expression, didn't help.

Nervously, she stepped away from the half-opened door, not daring to look inside in case she saw, or heard, Lindsey. 'I just meant, I hope you've got a clean shirt for Tuesday night,' she gabbled, a smile forced onto her stiff lips. 'Graham will be all dressed up, I'm sure, and we mustn't let him down, must we? Well, I'll be off. Cheers, Pete . . . '

She literally ran down the narrow street, only too well aware of the tall, brooding figure standing in the cottage doorway, watching her go.

★ ★ ★

The weekend passed without repercussion. Lindsey asked for advice about buying a dress for her forthcoming birthday party, and Gill was inveigled into going

146

off to Torquay on a shopping spree. The afternoon they spent together helped Gill to appreciate her new lodger's thorough niceness.

Once or twice she came near to mentioning Pete's name, just to see what the result might be, but each time her courage failed. It was better not to know, surely?

On Sunday evening, as she said goodnight to Lindsey, she said spontaneously, 'Don't forget that I meant what I said about your party — we'll have it here, and I'll help with the food. Can't have you fussing in the kitchen all the·evening . . . '

Lindsey paused in the drawing-room doorway, her face soft and pleased. 'I haven't forgotten. It's great of you. And yes, please, I'd like to have it here . . . '

'That's decided, then. We'll make plans in good time.' Gill smiled back. After the girl had gone upstairs, she sighed. Lindsey's birthday party would certainly answer the unasked question about her relationship with Pete. But there were still a couple of weeks to go . . .

Graham's dinner-party, Gill decided on Tuesday, was an occasion to savour. She dressed up accordingly, and when Lindsey's call from downstairs announced Pete's arrival, she knew she looked her best.

The plain, figure-skimming, sapphire-blue dress lent fire to her eyes and a new gloss to her shining fair hair. And the expressions on the faces that watched her descend the stairs left her in no doubt of the elegance and suitability of her appearance.

'Gill — you look marvellous!'

'Thanks, Lindsey. Not too much, is it?' Gill somehow avoided Pete's obviously admiring eyes, and smoothed the clinging material over her hips before putting on her sheepskin coat.

'No, just right. Golly, wish I had your figure!'

There was friendliness on Pete's face as he offered his arm, saying teasingly,

'My lady's carriage awaits. Or my old banger does . . . let's go, shall we? And mind the puddles. It's raining again, just for a change.'

★ ★ ★

The old car wheezed reluctantly up the hill out of the village, shuddering spasmodically as bursts of wind swept through the spaces between the houses lining the road. The windscreen-wiper made so much noise that Gill held her tongue.

She had planned to do her best to charm Pete this evening, possibly even getting him to tell her of his secret feud with Graham, but clearly this wasn't the moment. She hoped, rather anxiously, that things would improve as the evening wore on.

And they did. From the moment that Pete escorted her across the vast, gravelled drive outside Graham's house, Gill felt a lightening of her thoughts. Beneath the glare of the neon-lit porch, she appraised his appearance and saw how handsome he looked in a well-cut, dark-blue suit that emphasized the vividness of his eyes. A tingle of sheer pleasure raced through her as he took her hand, pulling her towards him in a brief moment of intimacy before the large front door opened.

'Got to cling together tonight, love,' he whispered wryly. 'You and me, versus Graham. Ah well, 'twas ever thus . . .'

'I won't let you down.' Gill pressed his fingers in return. 'I never did before, did I? And nothing's different now . . .'

A uniformed maid smirked at them from the archway of light that beamed out into the darkness. 'Good-evening. Please come in. Graham is expecting you.'

Ushered into an opulent cloakroom, all pink damask and mirrored walls, Gill hung up her coat and inspected her appearance very carefully. She was already amused at the pretentiousness of Graham's household, and was agog to experience more. But she needed to know that she looked her best.

She looked a typical London executive, composed and elegant, with a pleasant expression held firmly in place to hide the interest that surged inside her. For some unknown reason, she felt wildly excited. Instinct told her that the few hours ahead might well reveal unexpected facets of her cousin's complex character. And she would have Pete beside her all evening long . . . no wonder she looked radiant as she went out to find her host and his other guests.

The waiting maid took her into a brilliantly lit room where glass chandeliers, like drops of shining tears, glinted down upon an amazing amalgam of old and ultra-modern furniture and fittings.

But there was no time to stand and stare; Pete moved forward to join her at once, his quick, brief smile providing her with an extra surge of pleasure.

Behind him, Graham's near-set eyes caught hers.

'So there you are, Gill — my word, got your glad rags on tonight, eh?'

The usual cousinly *bonhomie*, thought Gill drily. Her smile tightened a little at the unnecessary sarcasm, but then she saw Brigitte Leconte standing at the end of the room and went down to greet her with unfeigned warmness.

The *petite* figure, dressed in a simple black dress that screamed of Parisian *haute couture*, turned and smiled in such a welcoming manner that Gill's momentary irritation with Graham faded immediately.

'I am so very pleased to see you again, Miss Wayland.'

'Oh — Gill — please!'

'As you wish. And I am Brigitte. Graham tells me you have moved from London, yes? And you are settled in by now?'

Gill smiled, a little pensively. 'Yes, thanks. At least, the furniture is settled . . . it'll take me a bit longer to do so,

I think. I miss the noise of the city, the people, my old job . . . '

Suddenly aware of how, unbidden, the words had spoken themselves, she stopped. Was it true that she really did miss London so much?

Brigitte put a sympathetic hand on her arm. 'I know how you must feel. I could never live in such a quiet, small place . . . and I miss France, too. Even with Graham, who is so kind, so thoughtful — '

She looked over Gill's shoulder to where Graham stood, and her dark, huge eyes were suddenly filled with something that made Gill tremble. She had never expected to hear Graham given such unspoken, but certain praise.

As if Brigitte read Gill's thoughts, her smile grew more pensive, her gaze left Graham, and she added quietly, 'Oh yes, he is a nice man, your Graham, but like all men he is — what do you say? — a little demanding at times! I must do this when he says . . . ' Her vital face took on a mischievous pout. 'And I must *never* do that . . . '

The tiny hands gestured in a most eloquent way and Gill wanted to laugh in sympathy. She felt a wave of friendship being generated between the two of them. Previously, she had regarded Brigitte Leconte merely as a rich man's daughter, over-indulged and selfish, but now she realized Brigitte had a mind of her own. And an almost English sense of humour . . .

'Graham has always wanted to be in charge,' Gill said quietly, with a humorous shrug. 'That's why he and Pete used to fight so hard. Why he was always in trouble with his father, who was a very domineering man . . . ' She halted, as Graham's hand possessively slid around Brigitte's bare shoulders, and his eyes challenged Gill's.

'Talking about me? Thought I heard my name. What's she been telling you, Brigitte? Don't believe a word of it, whatever it was! Gill's always been the clever-clogs who could leave me with egg on my face . . . '

Gill stiffened, taken aback. 'I didn't! You make me sound absolutely ghastly! Pete — come here and stand up for me. Graham's casting nasty aspersions . . . '

Swiftly, Brigitte turned her lovely face to smile pleadingly at Graham. 'Don't let's have a family row tonight, *chéri*? Please?'

Gill was very conscious of the brief silence that followed. She felt Pete come to her side, saw Graham's testy expression slowly fade, and knew a moment of utter relief as the maid approached with a silver tray of drinks.

'Ah! Champagne cocktails. Your favourite tipple, my darling.'

Putting a crystal glass into Brigitte's hand, Graham was all smiles again. After the initial toasting of their first drinks, he led the way into a glass-covered garden room that seemed to hang out in the enveloping darkness of the night several metres above the invisible garden, and, Gill worked out, many hundred metres above the nearby cliff face.

Brigitte looked out into the distance. 'If we opened the window, we could smell the sea . . . ' Swiftly she turned, smiling at Graham and putting her hand on his arm. 'Just a quick sniff, *chéri*! You know how I love to smell the salt . . . '

'No,' Graham said shortly. 'It's a nasty night, and I'd rather not think about the sea. Much pleasanter here, on dry land, with pleasant company and even pleasanter champagne . . . '

Brigitte shrugged and moved away petulantly. 'I shall never know why you choose to make boats when you are so afraid of the sea — '

'That's a lie!' Graham's quick-tempered response shocked Gill. She watched Brigitte shrug off the unpleasant words and direct her attention to Pete, at once asking him something about *Melinda II* and soon becoming engrossed in his reply.

Graham sidled across the room until he stood beside Gill as she carefully examined the hot-house shrubs and flowers that filled the garden room with an almost suffocating perfume.

'She doesn't understand,' he complained in a low voice. 'Just because, she hasn't got a nerve in her body, she reckons I'm the same. But I've seen too much of what the sea can do . . . storms, wrecks, drownings . . . '

Mystified, Gill watched a shiver strike through his entire body. He looked at her, almost pleadingly. 'Why can't she understand? She's a lovely girl, she's rich, she's got wonderful taste, and yet we've got this one barrier. The sea. The damned sea . . . '

Carefully, Gill made her voice very casual. 'We all have our little foibles, Graham. Brigitte probably has one that you haven't discovered yet. And if she loves you, she'll eventually understand how you feel . . . '

'Mmmm. Let's hope so.' Graham sighed, and for a moment Gill saw in his fleshy, mature face, the timid, difficult boy of their childhood. A feeling of uncomfortable compassion surged through her. She hadn't realized that he was like this, underneath all the ambition and delusions of grandeur. Poor Graham . . .

'Well! Come and look over the house. Can't wait to show you the house. Can't wait to show you the gallery upstairs . . . pictures are a great love of mine, you know. Remember how I used to sketch, as a boy? Come on, Gilly, this way — '

Alone together, in the subtly lit gallery that filled the north side of the entire upper floor, Gill followed Graham as he led her from picture to picture.

'And then this is my latest acquisition — Turner, — of course . . . '

His voice tailed off and she watched, fascinated, how he stood back admiring the painting of a ship in a troubled sea, lit by glowing sunlight that broke through massed, heavy cloud.

For this was a Graham she hadn't known before, a man who clearly found solace and beauty in works of art rather than in the reality of life. How could she ever again think of Graham as bad-humoured, sly and coldly ambitious?

He turned briefly to look at her and smile. His face was happy and relaxed. 'It's worth everything to me to have all this up here. When things get bad I come and look. And look . . . '

Gill was unable to reply. She was afraid that trite words might shatter his composure, banishing this new aspect of him. Nodding, she just returned his smile and hoped he would go on talking, revealing himself. But, as if his mind read hers, suddenly a shutter came down over his face.

The old expression of wariness returned, and she saw tension harden his fleshy jawline. Even his voice changed, dropping back to the petulant, rather bitter tone she knew so well.

'Yes. Well — we all have our fancies, don't we? And mine is rather more expensive than most . . . ' He stepped away, looking down the length of the gallery suspiciously.

'Seen enough, have you? Let's go down to the others, then. Good heavens, is that the time?'

An abrupt glance at his watch made an anxious frown settle on his face. He muttered something about a call coming through and then clamped his mouth firmly shut, looking at her apprehensively.

She followed him slowly down the ostentatious, wrought-iron spiral staircase to join in the light-hearted chatter going on between Brigitte and Pete in the sumptuous garden room overlooking the invisible sea.

★ ★ ★

Soon they all went in to dinner, on a gale of easy laughter, and Gill relaxed. Everything was, after all, all right. There would be no more drama this evening.

But she was wrong. Towards the end of the excellent meal, Graham was called away to answer the telephone.

Gill, sitting at his left hand, noticed instantly that he appeared to anticipate trouble. The way he left the table showed indications of anxiety; at the door he slipped on the polished parquet floor in his hurry to take the call. His voice wafted back to them, too high and pressurized to be natural — 'Carry on! I'll only be a minute — '

Across the table, Gill caught Pete's eye and then, at once, looked away again. She knew instinctively that if anything was to be done about following Graham to his study and listening to the telephone conversation, it must be her move alone.

Unlike Pete, now talking animatedly to Brigitte, she was the one who had the feeling that it was the mysterious Erik calling up Graham, and causing him such obvious harassment. And another thing; she knew now that her cousin's troubled mood was making her uneasy. She wanted, somehow, to help him . . .

Lazily, still listening to Brigitte's soft voice over the table, Gill rose to her feet.

'Excuse me, will you? Must have left my purse in the cloakroom when we arrived . . . stupid of me. Won't be a moment.'

She went quietly and unobtrusively out of the dining-room and then, in the octagonal hall, stood silent, listening for the sound of Graham's voice.

5

It was almost too easy to spy on Graham. Gill paused as she approached a closed door through which she could just hear his voice. She thought he sounded disturbed, almost shouting at the unknown caller. Without a second's consideration, slowly, and with infinite care, she opened the door a crack. It was enough to allow Graham's urgent words to swamp her mind.

'All right, all right! I told you I'd pay by the end of the month, and I will — but it's been difficult. Yes, Thursday evening, then . . . '

Silently, Gill closed the door and continued on her way to the cloakroom.

When she returned to the dining-table a little later, she met Graham's suspicious question with cool aplomb. 'Where've I been?' she countered smoothly. 'To powder my nose, of course! Did you think I'd been trying to pinch one of your pictures or something?'

Unexpectedly, Pete's voice chipped in, wry and good-humoured and obviously on her side.

'The feminine ego needs constant reassurance, as you must well know, Graham. Mirrors must be consulted at all times, faces repaired . . .'

Provoked, and with a note of challenge, Gill responded. 'So that's how you see me, is it? Merely a feminine ego? And I thought we sorted all that nonsense out years ago!'

She met his astute eye with a curious stare and was, once again, floored when he gave her the smallest, yet friendliest, wink possible.

'Only teasing, love. Actually, you're one of the nicest egos I know — hey, let's drink to that!'

She watched, placated, as with a smile he refilled their glasses, adding jocularly, and catching Graham's eye, 'To Gill and her ego!'

'And mine, too, please,' chimed in Brigitte, holding her glass high as she smiled up beguilingly into Graham's set face.

'What a lot of nonsense,' he muttered, but the harassed expression gradually faded as they all drank the foolish toast. Then relaxed laughter bound them together, and again they became at ease.

The evening wore on uneventfully and later they left the dining-room to return to the garden room, sitting and talking over coffee and brandy. Gill watched Brigitte, lounging beside Graham in a long, swinging cane seat, press closer to him, her small fingers unobtrusively seeking his hand, half-closed eyes demanding full attention.

For a second a dispiriting stab of pure jealousy racked Gill. Clearly Brigitte loved Graham. Such affection could not be masked. Reacting instinctively, Gill's eyes flew immediately to Pete, sitting a few yards away on a wrought-iron bench beneath a window hung in winter flowering jessamine.

She started, for he was already looking at her, a direct pensive stare, full of some emotion she was unprepared for. Her lips parted and she felt her breathing quicken. For in Pete's blue eyes was mirrored the same look she had just seen in Brigitte's. Love — but for whom?

Gill's head swam. This was absurd! Pete loved Lindsey — didn't he? Yes, it was obvious. Pete and Lindsey, both born and bred in Shelmouth, made for each other.

She held the vivid blue gaze with her own for a second more, before wilting beneath its force. She must get away, for she knew that love was not for her. Pete just happened to be looking at her as he thought about Lindsey . . . putting down her coffee cup, Gill heard it clatter on the table. She wondered vaguely if they could all see her hand tremble. But Brigitte and Graham were engrossed with one another. Only Pete still watched.

'God, that brandy packs a punch, Graham.' She staggered dramatically and heard them laugh. 'Can't see myself being bright and beautiful in the office tomorrow, the way I'm feeling! Come on, Pete, high time we moved, isn't it?'

Thank heavens for the practised sophistication which helped her climb out of the abyss of self-pity on which she balanced so unsteadily. Brilliantly, she smiled at them all in turn, and had the morose satisfaction of seeing Pete blink, as if a daydream had abruptly been, shattered. But he sounded his usual controlled self as he slowly rose, nodding across the room at her.

'You're right. What a terrible effect strong drink, good food and beautiful women can have on a man — '

She couldn't resist answering in the same flippant vein. 'Not to mention hothouse flowers and a full moon.'

'Very potent.' His voice was quiet, his gaze veiled now. So why should she feel as if he had meant far more than the two words conveyed?

Following his eyes as they left her face, she saw him look through the uncurtained windows to where, far beyond, between racing clouds, a silver orb glowed magically in the darkness, sending a comet's veil of vibrant reflection onto the limitless sea below.

A tingle travelled along Gill's blood and her disquiet died. For a moment she knew she and Pete were in absolute rapport: that, beneath their surface snaps and arguments, their shared affection was sure and constant, come what may.

They looked at the moon in its full beauty and then at each other, and there was no need to speak. Pete's eyes probed hers. He nodded slightly, and smiled, a gentle, understanding easing of set features, and she felt her own face respond, sliding into complete serenity.

Then the shared moment was shattered by Graham's voice invading it, his restlessness all too apparent.

'What's up with you two? Nothing to look at out there. Now, come on; before you go I want you to see the new jacuzzi I had put in last week.'

Obediently, Gill turned, stifling a sigh. She smiled warmly at her cousin, feeling her peace of mind making her more humane and sympathetic. 'You really are a trendy chap, Graham! I didn't know dear old Shelmouth had even heard of jacuzzis!'

Within the gleaming, white-tiled bath area, deep beneath the house, the admiring visitors were invited to sample the swirling water.

'No thanks,' Gill said decidedly. 'I like to bathe in solitude. But go ahead, Graham, don't mind me ... ' She raised an eyebrow as Brigitte, with a mischievous smile, waved a hand in farewell before disappearing in the direction of the luxuriously-furnished changing-room.

Pete nudged Gill as Graham's eyes followed Brigitte. 'Like you said, time to go,' he told her with a twinkle. 'I know when two's company and four's crowd.'

★ ★ ★

They left the house together, still seeming to share that earlier understanding. Gill shut her eyes as the car wheezed downhill and through the quiet village streets.

Strange how things turned out; she had been unprepared for this new sense of warmth generated between Pete and herself. It didn't enter her mind now to wonder if it could last. All that mattered was that it had happened.

The drive was too short, and she wished it might go on for ever. But before she expected, Pete was braking outside the looming shadows of The Lookout.

He turned towards her, and she sighed happily. 'What a lovely evening.' And then she stopped. In the half-light of the nearby streetlamp, she saw

Pete watching her, and knew she was a fool.

That look on his face — her stomach knotted and the old anguish returned, doubly severe now because she had all but forgotten its pain. He had a set expression, eyes dark and chill, and a sense of forbidding resolution emanated from him.

Without knowing quite what she did, she put out her hand. 'Pete?' There was no uncertainty in the manner he flinched at her touch and moved stiffly away. 'Give me your key. Gill — I'll open the door and see you in.'

Repelled, she clumsily opened the car door and scrambled out. 'No, I can manage. Thanks.'

On the doorstep she turned, knowing as she did so that this last appeal was foolish. 'Won't you come in? For a coffee? Or a nightcap?'

Standing by the car, just outside the light cast by the lamp, he was merely a tall, unrecognizable shadow. 'No, thanks. It's late.'

She swung open the door and stepped inside, wanting only to end the ordeal of their parting. 'Goodnight, then.'

★ ★ ★

Behind the shut door, she heard the car noisily drive away. She discovered she couldn't see because of the tears that filled her eyes. With an almost superhuman effort she wiped them away and went up to her bedroom, intent on forgetting the evening's events in instant, merciful sleep.

But still her agony of mind continued. For, just as, nearly thirty minutes later, she was at last drowsing, noises in the street below brought her sharply back to full and painful consciousness.

She heard whispers that were inaudible. A door — her front door — being opened and closed again with stealthy care. Indistinct footsteps walking away. Then a creak on the stairs and Lindsey's bedroom door admitting her.

Before Gill eventually slept, she had exhausted all but one of the many possibilities of these late-night sounds, and was convinced that it was Pete who had brought Lindsey home. Pete, suddenly anxious to get back from Graham's party, because he was meeting Lindsey later. There could be no other possible conclusion, she decided.

★ ★ ★

Gill awoke with a dragging headache. It was more positive to blame the wine and that last brandy than to put it down to emotional stress, which she knew to be the realistic cause. A couple of painkillers, a strengthening of her wilting resolution, though, and she was in the office as usual at one minute to nine o'clock.

Telephone and correspondence kept her occupied until lunchtime, but as she ate a sandwich in the kitchen, staring blindly out at the grey waters of the nearby harbour, her thoughts spread into a pool of remembered sadness.

The dinner-party. That strange moment of shared — what was it? — as she and Pete watched the full moon illuminate the blackness of the velvety night. Graham's words to the caller in that overheard phone call. Lindsey and Pete, saying goodnight at her front door.

Gill drank deep of her bitter and stimulating coffee, refusing to allow herself to mope any further. She was a self-assured, confident and efficient businesswoman.

She would cast aside her romantic and stupid feelings for a man who, plainly, sought love elsewhere, despite his friendliness towards her. Yes, cast them aside and forget.

With such resolution new ideas quickly sparked off. During the afternoon, she organized a search for a second-hand car. The local garage was quick to help, and as soon as she had locked the office behind her, she set off to inspect and test one of several likely vehicles.

She settled on a well-preserved and hardly-used white Mini, only some three years old. A far cry, she thought wryly, from the more up-to-date and opulent cars she had been used to when working in London and other far-flung cities. But it would do, making her completely independent.

No more relying on anyone — especially Pete, her mind nudged darkly — for lifts and car rides. And now she could drive herself to Heathway Creek on Thursday evening and find out exactly what game Graham and the mysterious Erik were up to.

★ ★ ★

Thursday was a cold, raw day with a blustering off-shore wind that turned the sea white with galloping horses of foam. But even after the sun had gone down, a certain luminosity from the waning moon provided light.

Gill, dressing warmly for her forthcoming adventure, knew she would be able to see all that she needed, amongst the shadowy scrub and copses of Heathway Creek.

The new car purred along confidently and some of her own optimism returned, although at the back of her mind the dark shadow of pain still lingered, ready to strike deeper should she let it do so. But, following the shadowy estuary along the winding, narrow coast road, she firmly pushed the memory of Pete far away from her. It was important to have a clear brain and an objective eye for this mysterious exercise she was engaged on.

So it was with a feeling of near-elation that she parked a little distance from the head of the creek, easily manoeuvring the Mini into a convenient patch of concealing darkness between an ivy-covered wall and the bulk of overgrown willow saplings. No one could possibly see it there.

Her breath was warm, misting the

cold air as she silently walked back towards the mooring-place of the unknown boat. She slipped into a handy hiding-place of old elm-stumps and twining brambles, discovering that she could comfortably perch on one of the tree-trunks as she peered through the concealing foliage.

Now it was just a question of waiting . . .

Slowly, the tardy minutes spun a misty, chilling web of reluctance around her. First her fingers, then her toes cried out as the cold reached them. She flexed muscles resolutely, but as her body grew more and more chilled, so her enthusiasm waned.

What on earth was she doing here? Probably catching her death of cold and running the risk of harassment, if not actual violence, should she be discovered.

The bleak image of Pete, fringing her mind, shifted and grumbled. What a fool she was. She should have told someone she was coming here, and

Pete was the obvious recipient of such dangerous information. If he were here with her, she would feel so much stronger — but he wasn't.

Her stiff face fell. He was probably with Lindsey, who had rushed in for a hurried meal and then, with stars in her eyes, gone out again, forgetting to even say goodbye.

Gill let out a sigh of utter despondency. All things considered objectively, and without the customary veil of emotion, she knew she'd been daft to come. So why not go home and forget Graham and his stupid, suspicious comings and goings? Home, where it would be warm and welcoming. She had left soup on the hob, and the remnants of a cold joint in the fridge . . .

Then a distant sound infiltrated her thoughts and she turned. She knew that noise — the unmistakable tremor of an approaching diesel engine. The boat, she thought with a mixture of sharp apprehension and excitement. Erik's boat, slipping in on the incoming tide, under cover of shifting clouds. It was actually here!

Recharged with new enthusiasm, all her lethargy died. Soon she could make out the shape of the boat, coming to a standstill in the mouth of the nearby creek. The engine died and again all was silent, save for a little flurry of bird cries — oyster-catchers disturbed at their nocturnal roost.

Concentrating hard, Gill saw a hazy figure appear on deck, bending as it fastened ropes to a mooring. Minutes later she heard a car drive up. There were hasty footsteps crunching along the road, and then muffled voices, too distant to be heard.

Graham! I'm certain it's him, she told herself urgently, and crept half-out of her hiding-place, the better to see and hear. But then the conversation faded and she realized both men had gone into the cabin.

Once more the night was quiet, broken only by wind slapping the tidal waters against the river-bank and causing foamy little waves to hush and shush on the sandy edges.

Gill's excitement retreated to a dull uncertainty. What should she do next? Beard the men on the boat? Try a citizen's arrest? The idea was off-putting. Erik had sounded dour and fierce on the phone and, as she well knew, Graham's obsessive anger could easily overbalance into violence.

She would be a fool to run such a risk. Her thoughts encountered harsh reality. She needed concrete evidence that anything illegal was going on on board the hidden boat, and so far all her suspicions were based on pure imagination.

The more she considered, the more ridiculous her presence here seemed. Yes, she would creep away and go home. Now. This very minute. Pulling a hooked bramble from her duffel coat, she stopped abruptly. Again, voices drifted to her hiding-place, and two figures emerged from the shadowy cabin.

This time she clearly heard Graham's voice saying roughly, 'OK, OK, I said I'd pay and I will. Good grief, I've just settled up for the last one, haven't I? Surely you can give me a bit of leeway with this new one. The end of next month, without fail. That do?'

The harsh, Scandinavian-accented reply was familiar, too. Erik, without a doubt. 'Only because you have been a good customer do I say yes, my friend. Four weeks today, the tide being right then. So long.'

They parted without ceremony, Graham climbing down from the boat and marching off towards his car, and the foreigner immediately returning to the warmth of the cabin. Gill knew the boat would remain hidden until the tide turned. No doubt Erik would pass the time cooking a meal and considering further plans.

She watched Graham passing the place where she hid, noting that he walked with a jaunty step, cradling a small, square package to his chest. Curiosity swelled and continued to grow as, after waiting another few minutes and hearing Graham drive off, she, too, returned to her car.

Exactly what was Graham up to? Definitely a shady deal of some sort.

Suddenly it was all rather depressing and frightening. Squalid, no longer exciting. She may have nurtured a childish hostility towards Graham in the past years, but now she knew better. Her cousin was clearly a tormented man, caught up in some illegal web of his own foolish making. She knew, with great certainty, that she wanted not just to unmask these activities, but to help him face them — and escape from them.

★ ★ ★

Contrary to her expectations, Gill found Lindsey at home when she returned to The Lookout, feeling tired and chilled through. The drawing-room fire roared a welcome, and a smell of fresh-roasted coffee wafted in from the kitchen, mingling with the soup she had left to warm.

Lindsey, rosy-cheeked and smiling, called out a quick greeting.

'Good timing, Gill. I've got the kettle on and I was just going to have some of that soup you made. Are you ready for a bite?'

'Yes, please. It's really cold outside.' Gill warmed herself thoroughly before collapsing in her customary chair.

Lindsey came in with a tray of sandwiches and stared.

'Where on earth have you been? You look like a ghost!'

'Oh — doing a spot of bird-watching, actually.'

Not exactly a lie; the oyster-catchers had been there! She ate her soup with enthusiasm and changed the subject. 'I thought you were out for the evening.'

'Only for an hour or so — went to see my parents.' Her face clouded briefly and she hurried on. 'But after that I — we — well — '

Something turned over deep inside Gill and she felt the colour fade from her cheeks. For even if Lindsey hadn't finished the sentence, the meaning was perfectly clear. She stared at the younger girl, who, smiling raptly, seemed to be radiating undiluted happiness. Yes, Lindsey's expression said it all.

She smiled down at Gill. 'It's a secret . . . ' But suddenly the words tumbled out. 'I've got to tell you! We're going to get married! Isn't it fantastic? We shall announce our engagement at the party.'

Gill's continued silence at last reached Lindsey. The pleasure fled from her expression. Anxiously, she sat down, staring across the coffee-table.

'I — I thought you'd be pleased,' she whispered. 'I know you like him — so what's wrong, Gill?'

Awareness came surging back into Gill's momentarily-frozen mind. She mustn't destroy this wonderful evening for Lindsey, even if her own hopes of happiness were now ground into the dust. Somehow she must bear this anguished moment, and all the moments ahead when Pete and Lindsey were together. Drawing a deep breath, Gill tried valiantly to regain some of the lost poise that had always carried the London-based Gill Wayland through crises and near-disasters.

If her hand trembled as she replaced the cup on the saucer, only she noticed it. Her voice somehow remained steady, warm and caring.

'I'm so pleased for you.'

And in that terrible moment she realized bleakly the truth of the trite words. If she couldn't have Pete, then the next best thing was that someone as genuine and lovable as Lindsey should. Pete's happiness was all that mattered, after all.

Her voice gained strength. 'Congratulations. I hope you'll both be wonderfully happy.'

Then it was only necessary to sit quietly and listen to Lindsey's voluble chatter about the forthcoming party. As soon as she could decently retire, Gill did so, pleading weariness. But the peace of her warm, quiet bedroom did nothing to comfort her or ease the overwhelming pain which the news of the engagement was causing her.

* * *

She sensed excitement surging through the boatyard the minute she reached the office next morning. Movement caught her eye, passing the interior window, and as she paused to wonder at the way the men were leaving their benches and workplaces, she suddenly knew the reason. Of course — *Melinda II* was being launched today.

A traditional excuse for bunking off and wasting a half-hour or so, the launch of a newly-built boat meant also that certain respected customs must be practised and revered.

Her mind abruptly sharpened by the sense of occasion, the grins on the men's faces and the sound of their raised, lilting West Country voices, Gill cast off the dull ache of pain that seemed to be permanently lodged somewhere in the depths of her body. She concentrated instead on the fact that this was a special day, celebrating the creation of yet another in the long line of sailing ships which had successfully started life as rough wooden keels, to be shaped, treated and built upon in the family boatyard.

A celebration. The word pushed itself to the forefront of her mind, and she clung to it gratefully. Despite her personal pain, she, too, would join in the happiness of this special day.

Putting on her anorak, she left the office, walking through the almost-deserted boatyard to the crowded slipway where *Melinda II* was moored. The men stepped aside with grins as soon as they saw her, and their unfussy friendliness cheered her on.

'This way, Miss Wayland; come over here, you'll be able to see better!'

Derek Hooker's arm gestured and his voice rose above the others. Gratefully, she allowed herself to be passed along the little groups of men until she stood next to him in a prime position where she could look down on the gently moving boat below without hindrance.

'What a lovely morning, Derek.' The sun was unbelievably bright and warm, and for once the wind was gentle, seeming only just strong enough to exercise the pennant flying on the mast.

'Tide's right, weather's right — good omens, Miss. The boat'll have a good life, with all this going for her.' Derek's all-seeing eyes were unexpectedly dreamy.

Gill asked curiously. 'Do you really believe that?' And he bent his head to meet her gaze with slightly shamefaced bravado.

'You bet I do! See here, Miss, boats is like birds — sorry, I mean girls, o' course. No knowing what they'll do next. So you gets a good sign at their launching, and everything's OK.

'Specially once the business with the seagull is over.'

'The gull? What on earth's that, then?'

But Derek didn't answer. Like everyone else, he was suddenly staring towards the back of the slipway, and Gill felt a silence sweep over the waiting men as she saw Pete approaching.

For a second her heart jumped. He looked so right, so personable, so at home in his thick navy sweater and shabby, water-stained jeans, his tanned face relaxed, fair hair shining like a beacon in the blinding spring sunlight.

He looked what he was, she thought, emotions choking; a man at home in his chosen environment of water, ships, and male workmates. But, then, curiosity calmed her, for in Pete's hand she saw the white feathers and handsome head of a captive bird — a gull of some sort. And then, with a leap into the past, she remembered.

Uncle Harry had instigated this odd, fey custom. Everytime a Wayland boat was launched, a seabird was thrown up into the air, its flight forecasting the reaction of the untried craft to the elements.

If the bird flew low and settled on the water, then the watchers on the quayside would be morose, for it meant a boat without purpose or stamina. But when the gull gained height and headed for the open sea, then all would be well and the boat's maiden voyage was blessed.

Just for a moment she imagined she saw Uncle Harry, stocky, tall, with that mop of greying hair, holding the captive bird at the prow of a boat, looking up into the heavens, saying something under his breath, and then releasing the struggling, independent creature into the wind.

★ ★ ★

The memory was broken by a bevy of voices calling her name. 'Miss Wayland, Pete's calling you.'

She looked down the length of the boat and saw him standing by the cabin door, beckoning her with his free hand and smiling a great, relaxed smile.

'Gill! Come here.'

She stumbled along the slipway and was helped aboard the swaying boat. 'What is it? What do you want?'

He didn't answer at once, simply lifted the captive bird and held it out to her.

Gill gasped. 'Me? You want me to do it? Oh, no . . . '

'Oh, yes. Graham's not here yet, and, anyway, he doesn't believe in the old customs. And the men would love to see a Wayland doing it — especially such a pretty one. Here, open your hands — careful, now . . . that's it. Remember what you say?'

'Remember? Oh!' Suddenly she did. The words came slipping back into her mind. She had heard them in her childhood so often as they came from Uncle Harry's lips. And now they were hers . . . to bless the boat, to put a final signature on the long-drawn-out contract of work that had kept the men in the boatyard busy for so long.

What a privilege Pete was handing her. Gratitude and happiness flowed into her, and without further encouragement she made her way to the prow of the boat, standing proud and relaxed just above the rolling grey waters of the harbour.

Silence behind her, and all around only the lapping waves and the busy, irritating cries of foraging oyster-catchers on the mussel-beds upriver.

Caught up in the magic of the moment, Gill lifted the struggling gull high in the air and gently threw it free. There was a murmur from the watching men, and then only her own voice, following the soaring wings of the gull. 'Ride the waves and tides and fly to your heart's delight. And always come home from troubled waters.'

Seventy pairs of eyes watched with intense joy as the bird gained height and strength, its wings making quick headway over the harbour and spreading estuary, and finally out to the sea itself. A good omen, indeed.

Gill sighed as a concerted shout of applause brought her back to reality. The pleasure all around her was infectious, and she smiled at the watching men. She had a lump in her throat. Being here meant so much. She had been right to come, after all.

Her gaze unself-consciously sought out Pete. He was standing at *Melinda's* cabin door, looking back at her and shouting. 'Gill. Have a look around before she's off — that's it, I've got you . . . '

With his hands safely supporting her, as abruptly the boat rolled from side to side, she was beside him, basking in the smile that he beamed down, momentarily forgetting Lindsey and feeling tremendously relaxed and happy.

'See what you think of the galley — not bad, eh?'

'It's great!' she said with enthusiasm. 'And, so efficient — hot-water heater, fridge, everything to hand and not an inch wasted; just like a suburban semi!' Smiling, she added wryly, 'You know, I'd almost trade in my kitchen at The Lookout for this . . . '

Pete looked at her with suddenly serious eyes, and a deeper note entered his voice, catching her attention at once.

'Would you? Would you really like to go to sea and live on a boat?'

'I — I — ' She turned away quickly, her serenity somehow spoiled by the change in his expression. 'Of course not,' she answered sharply. 'I'm a land girl. And, anyway, why should I go to sea? I've got a perfectly good home. And a job. I'm quite happy as I am.'

'Are you, Gill?'

Then, with immense relief, she heard approaching voices. 'Graham,' she said unevenly, and watched Pete's face settle into grim lines.

'Better late than never,' he muttered. 'We'd better go up — they'll be launching the boat any moment now . . .'

Without a word, Gill climbed back on board, immediately coming face to face with Graham, Brigitte, Neil Peters and his crewman.

'What're you doing down there?' Graham demanded, with his usual instant aggression.

Gill forced herself to smile disarmingly. 'Admiring your beautiful boat, dear cousin. She really is a smasher — Brigitte, you must be thrilled to think of *Melinda* as your very own . . .'

She merely nodded, but her vivacious face shone with agreement. Briskly, Graham said, 'Yes, well you're right, of course, Gill. *Melinda II is* a winner. Now, Neil, I want a word with you . . .'

He stumped off after the skipper, and

Brigitte's eyes twinkled at Gill.

'I am to do the launching,' she announced proudly. 'Here is the bottle, see?' A pout touched her perfect mouth. 'Such a waste of good champagne . . . ' Again the irrepressible smile burst out. 'But Graham and I will celebrate ourselves when we reach Cannes . . . '

'You're leaving this morning?'

'But yes. As soon as *Melinda* sails safely out of harbour.'

Something warm glowed in Gill's heart. Not envy this time, but enjoyable goodwill.

'I do hope your trip will go well,' she said impulsively. 'Not just *Melinda*'s voyage — but you and Graham, too . . . '

Brigitte leant forward and brushed Gill's cheek with her lips. 'Thank you,' she whispered. 'You understand, and you deserve to be happy, too. Oh, Gill, I do hope that . . . '

'Now stop nattering and let's get cracking!' Boisterously, Graham jostled Brigitte onto the slipway and back towards the stern of the boat.

Brigitte performed the ceremony of launching with charm and efficiency. Her voice rang out happily. 'I name this boat *Melinda II*. May God bless her and all who sail in her . . . '

The bottle cracked and the stern was afloat with champagne. A cheer went up from the watching crowd and the next moment, as moorings were slipped, *Melinda II* gracefully slid away from the boatyard slipway.

Through her memories and fears, Graham's voice called, loud with irritation, 'We're going, Gill — Brigitte wants to say goodbye . . . ' and she turned to say a last farewell, and to ask Graham for the key of the office safe.

Impatiently, Graham slid into the seat beside Brigitte in the waiting car outside the boatyard. He glowered. 'For heaven's sake. I shall only be gone for four or five days — everything can wait, can't it?'

Gill's smile died and her voice grew sharp. 'Not the men's wages. Of course

I must have the key. You can trust me not to reveal the secret combination, Graham . . . ' She forced a teasing note into the last words.

He frowned, looking like a sulky schoolboy. 'Oh, all right. I suppose you'd better have it.' Grudgingly, he handed over the key. Gill winked at Brigitte, who whispered soothingly in his ear, and the car shot off without further delay.

Slowly, Gill made her way back to the office. Everything seemed horribly empty and dull now after the shared excitement and satisfaction of seeing first *Melinda* leave Wayland's yard, and then Graham and Brigitte going off together.

When Pete came into the office minutes later, she was at a decidedly low ebb, and unable to stop her face and voice filling with affection as she looked up and saw him looking at her with an expression that instantly took her back to their shared upbringing.

'Poor little Cinderella left at home

alone?' he asked wryly, and she smiled, abruptly comforted.

'That's it exactly. The Ugly Sisters have gone to the ball and I'm here in the kitchen, with all the chores waiting . . . ' She gestured towards the pile of ledgers standing on Graham's desk, with the key to the safe sitting on top of them.

He was close beside her, gently easing her up from the chair. His smile was one of reassurance and strength and good-humour — and something else. Something that tugged at her wayward heart and would not be denied.

Because of his unexpected under-standing, the crowding memories of their previous closeness, and most of all because of his nearness, Gill gave in. Suddenly, she was in his arms.

6

It was true, Gill thought, floating in a glorious haze of joy, about seeing stars . . . and then thought was replaced by pure sensation. Pete's kiss seemed to last for ever, and it was only sheer breathlessness that finally forced her away from him.

Silently, they stared deep into each other's eyes. His arms were warm and secure, and she felt not just deliriously happy, but safe, in a way that reminded her of innocent childish contentment. Dreamily, she smiled into the familiar blue eyes that had now become dark pools of shared pleasure. Her heart beat even faster as she perceived desire grow in them.

He pulled her close again, and in that moment, unmasked, the image of Lindsey came into Gill's whirling mind. Lindsey, so young and sweet-natured, who didn't deserve to be cheated like this; whom they were both, undoubtedly, cheating by indulging in this extraordinary and wonderful spontaneous embrace.

Gill turned her head, and Pete's lips found her cheek instead of her mouth. She pushed wildly at his chest, levering herself away. Agonizingly she stared, watching the expression on his face change from simple enjoyment to a taut and critical surprise.

'What is it?'

She caught her breath, relieved that anger had come to replace the shattering knowledge of love.

'You ought to know!' Her voice was shaky and full of pain; turning her back, she stood looking down blindly at the littered desk.

Pete's hand, no longer gentle, pulled sharply at her shoulder, forcing her to face him again. 'Well, I don't. You'll have to tell me, I'm afraid.'

She could hardly bear the curtness of his words, the dark gleam of hurt rage in his smouldering eyes.

'Oh, come off it, Pete — it's hardly playing fair, is it?'

'Playing fair?' His voice rose in astonishment.

Miserably she watched as, slowly but irrevocably, scorn replaced the expression of surprise on his face. And then his words began to lash her.

'Oh, I see! Mustn't play games! Don't let's be naughty — is that it? And, d'you know, just for a second, I thought you were enjoying being kissed. Thought I'd actually cracked that cold, unfeeling shell you choose to hide behind . . . sorry, Gill, but you had me fooled, you know. Well, I won't bother you again, believe me — '

The disgust and anger in his voice, the contempt in his eyes, left her speechless and trembling. He stormed out of the room in a whirlwind of suppressed fury, the door slamming behind him, sending papers flying from the desk, and a badly-placed catalogue dropping out of the shelves that lined the far wall.

Not knowing what she was doing, Gill slowly retrieved the fallen objects, her mind a seething hotch-potch of thoughts, emotions and never-to-be-forgotten sensation.

She loved him. She would always love him, no matter what he said or did. But he belonged to Lindsey, and there was no way in which she would ever again allow herself to be seduced into such indulgence of stolen kisses. Didn't he know how she loved him? After that kiss — hadn't he guessed?

★ ★ ★

She wandered to the window, and looked out over the harbour. The tide was on the turn, gulls retreating from the mud flats upstream and flying, in slow and solemn formation, towards distant shorelines stretching hazily outside the estuary mouth.

The day that had begun so brilliantly,

with sun and spring-like warmth, was fast deteriorating into a typically treacherous late August disaster. Indigo clouds raced up over Dartmoor's far peaks, and an increasing wind spattered foam over the grey-green rolling waters.

The greyness outside matched the gloom of Gill's spirits. She sighed, and the lonely, despairing sound filled the room, returning her finally to the fact that self-pity would get her nowhere, and, anyway life went on.

A glance at her watch showed a good two hours until lunchtime. Time enough to get on with the waiting work. The ledger — that was the first task.

Returning to her desk, she forced herself to open the well-thumbed pages and concentrate on the figures that danced meaninglessly before her eyes.

And then, slowly, but with growing interest, she forgot about herself and Pete and Lindsey, about everything except the undeniable fact that there were many serious discrepancies here between entries, invoices, VAT demands, and bank statements.

'He can't be — not cooking the books. Not *Graham* . . . ' she said to herself. But after another half-hour's close scrutiny, she knew he was.

Wearily, Gill closed the ledger and leaned back in her chair, pondering the unpalatable truth which had just been so clearly revealed. For the last nine or ten months, Graham had been making false entries, all of them to his own credit, and therefore to the detriment of the business.

In a strange way, she wasn't completely surprised. Graham had obviously been short of money. Various incidents came back to her, now meaningful and serious. She recalled what he had said to Erik, only last night. *'I told you I'd pay by the end of the month, and I will — but it's been difficult.'*

Then she remembered his reluctance to allow her into the office; his grudging handing over of the key to the safe. Abruptly, she sensed that the safe might well contain even more incriminating evidence of shady deals and cover-ups.

She wrestled with its combination and then held her breath as, at last, the door opened.

Some pass-sheets lay on top of other papers; there was a wadge of banknotes and some bags of cash. Rapidly, Gill inspected the contents, paying special attention to the pass-sheets. She saw several large amounts paid in over recent months, figures far in excess of the monthly salary paid to Graham from the boatyard.

With a sinking feeling, she guessed these extra sums must balance the false entries in the ledger. She knew her next job must be to calculate them exactly.

But there was something else at the bottom of the safe — a small, square package that made her gasp, as she recognized its shape. For surely this was what Graham had been carrying when he left Erik's boat at Heathway Creek . . .

She carried it to the desk. There, beneath layers of careful wrapping, she discovered a magnificent oil-painting of a ship, tossing perilously on mountainous seas. Gill was sufficiently artistically knowledgeable to realize that she held a genuine Von Praken in her hands, worth thousands on today's acquisitive art market.

The truth was plain and depressing: Graham had become so obsessed by his passion for works of art that he had embezzled from his own family business funds, and was cheating not only the bank and the government, but herself and Pete, the minority shareholders.

Dislike Graham as she might, it was difficult to concede such criminal actions, but the proof lay all around her; her cousin was guilty of fraud.

Mr Hartland — he'll tell me what to do about this . . . the elderly solicitor's friendly face beamed into her mind like a ray of hope. It would be the greatest relief imaginable to share this ghastly trouble with a professional who could advise without prejudice.

But Gill was no fool; during her years of business experience she had learned that such advice must inevitably lead to putting matters into hands which needed to deal with them — those of the police.

Inspector Merrill, the local police chief, had been a long-established friend of the family. He and Uncle Harry had played golf together on innumerable Sunday mornings — could she go to him, perhaps, with Graham's problems?

No, of course not. The idea was repulsive. It would be tantamount to betraying him. Blood was thicker than water and, cheat or no cheat, surely he deserved a chance to repay his debts, and to clear his name, before taking such drastic measures?

Indecision racked Gill. She moved from desk to window and back again. The lunch-hour passed, unnoticed, and the afternoon slid by. The office grew dark and cheerless as the night-rack obscured the half-hidden frail sunset, and her own mind increasingly reflected the sombre atmosphere.

Abruptly, she made up her mind. Put away the incriminating ledgers and the treasured picture, close the safe, lock the office and go home. After all, she had five days' grace before Graham's return. Time enough in which to sort out all the possibilities of dealing with things.

Tomorrow she would face the problem anew. Right now she needed company and a drink before supper. Lindsey — she would go and find her, and in casual, relaxed conversation put behind her this nagging anxiety.

Gill's face lost its tautness, and she was smiling as she locked the office and the interconnecting door.

But The Lookout, although warm and as welcoming as ever, held no human company which might comfort her. Even as she went into the kitchen, Gill heard footsteps flying down the stairs and through the hall.

'Lindsey?' Her call was peremptory, and she regretted the hard tone the minute she saw Lindsey's surprised face turn and stare back along the passage, her hand still on the front door latch.

'Yes? What's wrong, Gill?'

She hadn't meant to sound like that; it was just disappointment at realizing that another lonely evening lay ahead of her. Carefully, Gill smiled and softened her voice, holding onto her self-control with the little strength left to her.

'Nothing. Sorry. I didn't mean to snap — '

Lindsey's pretty face showed immediate understanding. 'You're working so hard, and all on top of your move, too. You know, they say a move is as traumatic as a death or the break-up of a love-affair — '

Gill swallowed the lump that came into her throat. If only Lindsey knew how near the truth she was . . .

'Yes, well, I think I'll have an early night. I do feel a bit worn-out. Not much on the box, as I remember — er — going out, are you?'

An inane question. Of course she was going out — she wore a new, bright navy jump-suit and her frizzy hair was more carefully groomed than usual. And her eyes shone like stars.

'Yes. We're going to have supper at the Lobster Pot — haven't been there for ages.'

Briefly, Gill wondered why Lindsey never gave Pete a name; and then was thankful. Feeling as she did, it would press salt into the wound to keep hearing him talked about.

'I'll try not to wake you when I come in — sleep well and have a good rest, Gill. 'Bye.'

The door closed quietly and Lindsey was gone. Gill went back to the kitchen feeling wryly that she had been spoken to as if she was an elderly maiden aunt, safely tucked up for the night and then forgotten.

If only Lindsey knew.

Next day she awoke with the answer to the problem clear in her refreshed mind. Pete was the key to the whole thing, of course. She must tell him exactly what she had discovered about Graham and the money.

It would be difficult, even embarrassing, after that embrace, to actually seek him out and demand to talk business, but she saw it as the most constructive and positive step to take. For Pete knew Graham of old; knew him as well as she did. And he was, after all, a fellow shareholder, so Graham's fraudulent borrowing must affect him as deeply as it did her.

Gill ate breakfast with a return of her usual good appetite and made plans to see Pete with a feeling of relief. She had been very down last night — thank heavens the new day brought more confidence and hope with it.

Leaving the house in good time, she

put a note in Pete's office before the boatyard came to life. The note asked him to meet her for a drink that evening at a small pub just outside the village.

Please come, she had written urgently, *It's about business and very important.* It had been difficult to push aside the painful longing to see him that threatened to cloud her thoughts, but she had done so, and felt all the better for doing so.

Returning to the office, she immersed herself in work. Tallying the ledger with amounts paid into Graham's bank account resulted in the confirmation of her suspicions. The figures matched sufficiently for her to realize she had definite proof of his embezzlement.

With the long, busy day at last behind her, Gill set out in her car, hoping and praying that Pete would keep the date she had forced on him. On the seat beside her lay the carefully-packaged oil-painting she had found in the safe. If Pete needed proof of

Graham's activities, surely this would provide it.

★ ★ ★

The White Lamb was a little inn not often frequented by the fishing community in the village, who preferred to drink and chat in one of the many local pubs clustering around Shelmouth Harbour.

Gill parked the Mini, picked up the picture and went into the lounge bar, where a smoky fire and dim lighting greeted her. She was glad she didn't recognize any of the faces that idly looked up at her entrance. No one would know her here — or Pete, either, when he arrived. If he arrived . . .

She sat down in a shadowy corner on a creaking old oak settle, and sipped at a mediocre sherry, her thoughts racing. It was important that no local gossip-monger saw her here. Above all Lindsey mustn't find out that she and Pete had met. Even as she looked about her, Gill felt a vague stab of guilty unease. In picking such a shabby, out-of-town meeting-place, she had surely laid herself open to obvious accusations of deceit and secret assignation.

Then the door opened and Pete entered. He saw her at once, nodded, unsmiling, and went to the bar to collect a tankard of beer. Sitting down at the small table opposite her, he looked across with cold eyes. 'Are you ready for another drink?'

Just for a second it seemed her heart was in her mouth. But she remembered Lindsey, and somehow remained calm. 'No, thanks. I've hardly started this one.' She forced a brief smile. 'Not exactly my idea of a good sherry, anyway.'

'Not exactly an ideal place to find one. Couldn't you have picked somewhere slightly more up-market? This has always been a run-down pub.'

Pete took a long swig of his beer. Over the rim of the glass his eyes held hers and she found herself stuttering slightly as the need to explain surfaced.

'I — mm — I wanted — I mean, it seemed sensible to get out of the village . . . '

'Why?' He returned the glass to the table, sitting back in his chair and staring hard at her colour-drained face.

She took a long steadying breath before replying. She, too, leaned back, feeling the hard wood of the settle firm against her drooping shoulders. The support helped and the words came then without thought as she faced his almost-accusing gaze.

'Because what I've got to tell you mustn't be overheard. Pete — '

Conscious of having at last interested him, she leaned forward slightly, her voice low but growing more confident and sure.

'I've been doing Graham's books and it's quite clear that he's embezzled some money. Thousands of pounds, actually. It's been going on for about ten months. I found various papers in the safe, proving that he's defrauded the business. And I found this, too . . . '

She took the package from where it had been hidden on her lap, and began unwrapping it.

Before taking the last piece of paper from it, she looked up at Pete again. His expression hadn't altered, and he hadn't spoken, but she knew him so well; knew that all she'd said was being silently considered and that he would make no comment until he'd decided whether to accept her words or not.

Hesitantly, she smiled at him.

'Look, I'd rather not put this on the table and show it to the world at large. It's — well, valuable, to say the least. Could you come and sit round here, beside me? Then no one can see.'

He moved without comment, sitting close, yet apart, his presence a sudden torment to her. She cleared her throat and tried to concentrate on the picture as she pulled aside the last covering.

'It's Von Praken's 'Storm at Sunset'.

Graham's been buying some other old masters from this Erik chap — he's a Dane, I think; you know, the one who phoned and asked Graham to meet him at Heathway Creek.'

She sensed Pete's disapproval suddenly flare, and caught her breath.

'Good grief,' he said caustically. 'So you went and watched. Didn't you?'

Turning, she found the blue eyes accusing her like twin laser beams. She stumbled for words.

'Y-yes. I did, but — but only because — '

'Well? Because of what?'

Her thoughts came tumbling out unchecked. 'Because you weren't interested — or helpful. Because I thought *you* thought I was being stupid — '

'And, my God, so you were. *Stupid*?'

His low voice rose a tone and made her shrink. Guilt and remembered fear ran through her; those awful moments, lurking in the midst of the estuary; the realization of the danger she had so foolishly placed herself in . . .

'You were crazy to go on your own,' he went on remorselessly. 'Anything could have happened. You know what Graham's like when he's angry — if only I'd known what you were up to . . . '

Amazed at the heat in his usually controlled voice, Gill could only stare as he snatched the picture from her and held it beneath a subdued lamp on the window-sill nearby.

She'd known, of course, that he would disapprove of her attempt at detective work, but this was something deeper and more frightening. She felt as if Pete had more personal interest in her ridiculous scheme; as if he thought she had done it merely to upset him.

'Look,' she said quickly, 'I know it was a daft thing to do; I knew as soon as I got there that I was laying myself open to all sorts of dangers, but Graham is *my* cousin. OK, we have our differences, rows even — but, well, he's family . . . '

She tailed off as a dark eyebrow rose in cynical astonishment. Pete's expression made her defend her words.

'I haven't got anyone except Aunt Mary and Graham.' She heard her voice grow edgy and thin as her self-control threatened to fade.

'I need the few family ties I've got left. It's a big, hard world out there, and sometimes I'm lonely . . . '

Her hands clenched into fists and abruptly she wished she was indeed a helpless little woman, who could cry and beg for help.

But she wasn't that sort, never had been, never could be. All her life she'd been independent, fighting for what she wanted, earning her achievements. Her thoughts raced back into antagonism. '*So, damn you, Pete Oakridge! Stop looking at me as if I were a hysterical child. I can manage without you, or anyone . . .* '

The bitter, challenging statement swept through her like a sweeping wind, clearing away the self-pity that she hated and denied. And, even as she damned him, an errant sense of the ridiculous returned, bringing relaxation and a smile to her tense face.

Suddenly, she was able to meet his penetrating stare with confidence. Yes, she loved him, although he would never know it, and it was important to show him that she was a woman worthy of admiration and approval, after all.

'Call me a fool if you like,' she told him coolly, 'but I intend to give Graham a chance to repay his debts. He'll be back here in another four days and then I'll tell him that I know everything he's been up to. In the meantime, I'll find out the exact value of this . . . ' She held out a hand for the picture . . . 'so that he can put it to auction without delay. That alone should clear most of the backlog of debts.'

The look on Pete's face made her voice die away. It was there again, the old steely, secret hatred, which she had so feared from the first days of their reunion. Uneasiness surged, and she said sharply, 'Give it to me, please, Pete.' But her hand remained hovering over the table, unfilled.

Wide-eyed and disbelieving, she watched him rewrap the picture, carefully putting it on the settle at his far side, well out of her reach.

He glanced at her. 'You're a fool, Gill,' he said, and now he sounded almost friendly. As if they were back in the past, and she had done something silly and he had covered up for her . . .

'Fancy trying to get a mean, conniving moron like Graham out of the trouble he's set up for himself. I thought better of you. Believe me, he isn't worth bothering with. And I'm not going to let you get involved in all his wretched affairs.'

Stung beyond endurance at such lack of understanding and sympathy, she snapped back at him. 'I'll do whatever I want, without asking your consent, thanks very much!'

Rising, she reached across him, intent

only on retrieving the picture. But he was too quick for her. His hands snatched at hers and she was caught, unable to move, very close to his seated body. Close enough to see his eyes abruptly grow deep and intense. Close enough to feel his breath on her cheek.

A silence more poignant than words stretched between them for a long moment. His hands were hard about hers, but they were warm and secure, Gill drew in a quavering breath, 'Let me go, Pete. Please — '

She closed her eyes rather than look into his and see again — or had she only imagined it? — that spark of growing desire that forced her reluctant thoughts back to the day they had kissed.

'Please,' she whispered again, and then was desolate because he had done as she asked. He was on his feet, standing well away from her, the package safe, tucked beneath his arm.

'Do what you want, Gill.'

She'd never heard his voice so low and impersonal. It was as if that moment between them had never happened. The thought seared her.

Standing erect, she pulled on her coat, shouldered her bag, and walked rapidly past him towards the door. 'I certainly will. And without your help, thanks very much.'

It was an enormous relief to get out into the bracing freshness of the cold night. She walked across the yard to her parked car and was unlocking the door when footsteps crunched behind her. Whirling around, she stared into Pete's sombre face.

'One last word, Gill,' he said quietly. 'Stop prying in matters that don't have anything to do with you. Graham deserves to get his comeuppance, and I'm not going to let you stop it happening. So go home, like a good girl, and forget all about the books. And about this — '

In the shifting moonlight she saw him touch the package he held. Then, before she could argue, or try to get it from him, he was gone, a tall, blurred shadow swiftly disappearing from view.

★ ★ ★

Alone, Gill got into the car, slumping wearily behind the wheel. She felt deflated and let down. She had been so sure that Pete would understand and help, but things had gone from bad to worse. Not only had she betrayed Graham's secrets, but the valuable Von Praken had gone and, perhaps more disastrous than anything else, Pete had clearly shown that he thought her a weak and stupid fool.

She drove on aimlessly, down dark, twisting lanes that led to remote hamlets and solitary farmhouses, and eventually into a wilderness of heath and scrub, shadowy and fearsome in the racing moonlight. Her thoughts churned and tumbled. Somehow, she must find a way out of this ghastly turmoil of family problems and lingering passions; and she herself must do it, with no help from anyone, let alone Pete.

Later, she discovered she was driving along the estuary road, close to Heathway Creek. On impulse she stopped the car by the copse where she had hidden previously.

Sitting there in the darkness and solitude, she heard again the oyster-catchers' cries, smelt the salt in the air as the wind rolled in from the sea, and wondered at the mess her world was in.

And then, out of the blue, the answer came. It was so quick, so obvious, that she laughed aloud as it shot through her. 'Of course! What a fool I've been! *I'll* buy that wretched picture myself and help Graham pay back the money! The Lookout, yes, I could sell that and move somewhere smaller and cheaper . . . '

But no, Uncle Harry suddenly seemed very near and she knew that to sell the old house would be betraying all the

cherished memories and hopes that he
had entrusted to her.

Mortgage the property? The idea
didn't appeal. She could just hear Mr
Hartland's precise voice reminding her
of family loyalties. 'All right, then. I'll
raise the money some other way.'

In the silence her voice sounded
harsh and unfamiliar. She sat on in
the car, staring blindly into the windy,
shadowy night outside, and knew that
she had come up with the only possible
solution.

Her shares in the boatyard carried no
ties. Unlike the house, they could be
disposed of without any recriminations.
Especially if she sold them to Pete! Gill
gasped. No, not sold. *Gave them to
him in return for the painting*.

Yes! That was it, the way not only
to help Graham, but to ease herself out
of this torture of living and working
so close to Pete. A torture that could
only increase once he and Lindsey were
married.

She would give Pete her shares in

return for the Von Praken. Sell it, and enable Graham to repay what he had taken from the business. Then move away from Shelmouth, renting out The Lookout, and possibly returning to her old life in London.

It was a drastic step, and one she had never envisaged taking, not since discovering how content she felt at Shelmouth, but now it seemed the only sensible thing to do.

Gill switched on the ignition and drove home. There would be a lot to do tomorrow and she needed a good night's sleep before then.

★ ★ ★

As she had anticipated Mr Hartland clearly disapproved of her decision when she telephoned him the next morning, but he had no authority to forbid it. His voice brought memories of Uncle Harry, and she had to steel herself to remain resolute.

'I've thought this through very

carefully, Mr Hartland.'

Just for a second she hesitated, but the words came smoothly and with only the mere vestige of untruth. 'It's been pleasant to be back in Shelmouth, but quite honestly things haven't turned out quite as I'd hoped.' She smiled wryly to herself; that at least was very true.

'And so it seems sensible for me to cut my losses and return to London. I have friends there, business contacts — I'm sure I shall settle down again without much bother.'

'But selling your shares, my dear — is that necessary? I mean, do consider the family connection . . . ' His pleasant voice held an edge of disappointment.

'I'm sorry but I've made up my mind, Mr Hartland. Perhaps I haven't made myself quite clear; I'm not selling the shares — I want them transferred to Pete Oakridge.'

In the momentary silence, she visualized the solicitor's surprise and curiosity. But he merely replied, rather gruffly. 'Very well, if that's what you've decided. I'll draw up a deed of gift.'

For some reason Gill found it necessary to explain further. 'It's — it's a wedding present,' she elaborated, and then wished she'd held her tongue. But Mr Hartland's professional ethics forbade any more questions.

'I see,' he said impersonally. 'Well, Miss Wayland, I'll be in touch as soon as the deed is ready for your signature.'

'Thank you, Mr Hartland. Goodbye — '

She felt enormously relieved as she replaced the receiver. The die was cast. She had actually done it. All that remained now was to persuade Pete to give back the painting, in return for the shares.

Her heartbeat quickened as she faced the undeniable fact that there was bound to be a difficulty, when the moment came to face him again. Supposing he refused to accept her shares? He could be extremely awkward when he wanted to.

Gill crossed the office and went to the interior window, staring down into the yard. It looked a hive of activity and despite her uneasiness, a small burst of pleasure went through her as she watched the carpenters at work on the new keel, laid down only two days ago as the result of an order from a shipping magnate in Guernsey, for which she had been wholly responsible. Her business acumen still flourished, it seemed.

She sighed and returned to her desk. How long would it be before all this was just a memory, and she would be back in London, once again filling her life with a new career, a new home, and the old friends whom hopefully, had not quite forgotten her? Would it all make up for the loss of the boatyard? Of The Lookout? Of Pete . . .

It was hard to put a smooth face on and pretend all was well. In a way, Gill was glad that Lindsey was invariably out each evening and that certain arrangements for the forthcoming party had been left in her hands. It helped fill up the long, desolate evenings when she was alone with her thoughts.

Aunt Mary had the flu, so Gill drove around to her house at lunchtime the next day to see what she could do for the invalid.

'Now, you just stay there — you should have let me know when you didn't feel well,' Gill scolded, as she took some soup and sandwiches up into the small bedroom beneath the eaves of the old thatched cottage.

Her aunt looked small and pale beneath the faded patchwork quilt. She smiled fondly.

'You're a good girl, Gill. It's lovely having you here. But I didn't want to trouble you. I mean, you're so busy in the office, and with Graham away as well . . . '

'You're far more important than the silly old office,' Gill answered quietly, surprised how deeply she felt the truth of her reply.

Aunt Mary, frail and helpless, was suddenly a much-needed member of her small family. She wished, too late, she could spend more time here in the little cottage, talking about her past childhood and strengthening the ties that still held them together.

★ ★ ★

Back at work that afternoon, having done some shopping and washing for her aunt, Gill regretted the long years spent in London building up her career, when she could have been visiting Shelmouth, enjoying both Aunt Mary's and Uncle Harry's company.

Then the painful thought came that, had she returned to Shelmouth earlier in their lives, maybe Pete would have loved her and not Lindsey — but that was too desperate to consider any further. She forced herself back to the ledger yet again, to assess the amount she must raise to pay off Graham's debts.

At teatime she heard Pete's voice directly outside the office door and held her breath, but he didn't come in. Clearly, he was avoiding her.

She sighed. Well, she couldn't blame him — but the moment was drawing near when she must seek him out and hand over the deed of gift of her shares in the business. She knew she was dreading it . . .

Just before leaving the office, Mr Hartland's secretary rang to say the document was ready for signature and would she call in tomorrow at 10.15 a.m.

Gill marked the appointment in her diary, not sure whether to be glad or sorry. Was she betraying Uncle Harry's trust in her, after all? Surely not — for he had looked upon Pete as another son, and so would understand the reason for the change of ownership of the shares.

★ ★ ★

With the deed duly signed and safe in her bag, Gill left Mr Hartland's office next morning. He had been polite but briefly dismissive. Clearly, he considered she was indulging herself at the cost of family loyalty, although no such words had passed his lips.

Gill's own mouth was tightly set as she drove back to Shelmouth. She supposed she must get used to this unpleasant knowledge that, once the news of her withdrawal from the business was out, the local gossips would weave their usual illusory web of fairytales with malicious enjoyment. Ah well, she would be gone soon. She told herself sharply that she knew what she was doing; that keeping the family name intact was all that mattered.

Through her, Graham's secret would remain hidden. But was that *all* that mattered? She began wondering what Lindsey would think — how Graham would react — and; above all, what would Pete say when she confronted him with her decision?

But her sense of personal anxiety died the moment she stepped into the office. Pete himself came striding up from the yard, his face dark with anger, his mind obviously too full of the news he'd just received to feel any lingering animosity from their last meeting.

'Trouble with *Melinda II*,' he told Gill quickly. 'Just had a message from Neil — he's heading back for repairs. God knows what's wrong. Graham's coming back, too.'

'Engine trouble?' Gill asked hopefully. Business would deteriorate if *Melinda*'s plight was anything to do with the basic construction of the boat, whereas a fault in the engine could be replaced with no harm done.

'Sounds more like a mess-up with the stabilizers,' Pete growled. 'I told Graham he was a fool to insist on that extraordinary idea of his — I mean, we had enough trouble with the first *Melinda* on that score. Why couldn't he learn from the boat going down and Dad drowning, for God's sake?'

Gill shook her head, uneasy at his obvious resentment and rage.

'When will he be back?' she asked, as Pete headed for the door.

He shouted briefly over his shoulder, 'Midday tomorrow.'

Alone, Gill surveyed the new disaster with a sinking heart. So much had depended on this new boat . . . she knew, too, that she must get her own plan into operation before Graham returned. That meant she had only the rest of the day and the next morning in which to see Pete and get back the painting.

'I'll see him tonight. The sooner I can talk to him the better.' Her thoughts were brave enough, but as the afternoon wore on her anxiety grew, and her hands trembled as, later that evening, she packed up the small bundle of share certificates, together with a copy of the deed of gift, and set off to see him.

There was a light on in Pete's cottage at the far end of the curving promenade.

Gill parked a little way off, locked the car and then walked up the cobbled street. She had practised, all afternoon, exactly what she should say to him, but now her mind was a blank.

Only one thought came, repeating itself over and over again as she stood by the front door, hand raised to lift the door-knocker.

'I hope to goodness Lindsey isn't here, with him — '

7

Despite Gill's already nervous anticipation, she was startled when the door opened and Pete stared out from the light-filled cottage.

She saw his surprise and waited, with her hands clenched around the envelope of share certificates, for annoyance, even anger, to turn his eyes dark and hostile. But he smiled pleasantly, pulling her in out of the cold darkness.

'Come on in, you look like an orphan in a storm — what's up, love?'

Love. That word again. For a moment she shut her eyes to try to escape from all that it meant; but he was leading her towards the fireplace, helping her off with her anorak, and she stared down at the flames licking lumps of driftwood as, silently, she sat down.

'You'd better have a drink. I've never

seen you looking so pale — feeling OK?'

He went to a cupboard and produced a bottle and glasses.

Her teeth had begun to chatter.

'A noggin will do you good. Here, drink this — '

Gill did so reluctantly, then leaned back in the chair, which she recalled had been his father's favourite seat by the fire. Slowly, relaxing warmth swept through her, helping her to untie the knot of tension this visit had caused.

Pete sat on the edge of a chair opposite, leaning forward with a glass between large, work-scarred hands, and she was encouraged by the expression of obvious concern on his face.

Just for a moment she allowed herself to look at him in close detail. This old sense of companionship and rapport would never last, once she told him why she was here. So look at him now, and remember.

Tousled, weather-bleached hair, curling behind his ears. Of course he would get it cut before the engagement party. Hooded, deep eyes above prominent cheekbones, and that high-bridged, proud nose that they had joked about as children. The 'Oakridge nose' Pete had called it, grinning. And then his mouth . . .

Gill sat up very straight, blinked and forced wayward thoughts back to the reason for being here. 'Look,' she said shakily, 'I've come to make you a proposition. About last night — '

He cut through her words quietly, but decisively, and she wondered if she was hearing right.

'If you hadn't come here I was going to call on you this evening. To apologize about last night. I'm sorry, Gill — I was no help to you. And I was damned rude, too. Forgive me?' he suggested ruefully, and she saw a gleam of wry humour softening his blue gaze.

What could she say? It was impossible to have any lingering feelings of acrimony in the face of such an abject apology. She let out her breath in a long sigh and began weakly to laugh.

'Of course I do. But — but you're so — I don't know, unexpected and . . . '

'Hopeless?' It was a familiar, childish term of abuse and she could only grin back at the strong, smiling face that confronted her.

'Absolutely hopeless. You'll never change!'

'I should hope not.'

The fire crackled as if in imitation of their unrestrained laughter and Gill forgot everything except how marvellous it was to be here, warm and safe, with Pete. She watched him get up, take her glass and head for the tiny kitchen. His voice reached her over the clatter of pans, and the slow sizzle of frying fat.

'Stay where you are. I've got a meal half-cooked. I bet you haven't eaten anything lately — you know, you've lost weight since you came home, Gill.'

Home. Another loaded word. And he'd noticed how thin she was getting;

not surprising, with all the worry, and hardly complimentary of him to mention it, but — he'd noticed. Gill blinked rapidly and forbade her errant feelings to get the better of her.

'Don't tell me it's fish-fingers again?' she said brightly.

'Naturally. But tonight I'm putting on three courses, especially in your honour. Look in the cupboard beside you and find a tin of soup, will you? Tin-opener here, in the drawer by the sink . . . '

It was easy now to get up and stand shoulder to shoulder at the cooker and talk as freely as they once used to, in childhood's unclouded days. In fact, so easy had the atmosphere become that Gill heard herself drifting into a fatal mistake.

'You and your fish-fingers! I bet you had something a bit more complicated at the Lobster Pot, didn't you?'

Her voice tailed away, as realization stabbed, and she awaited his reply with a dismal foreboding. How could she have been so foolish as to break this glorious friendliness by bringing Lindsey into it?

But Pete's voice was as casual as ever. 'Can't remember what I had; it's such a long time ago.'

Thankfully, Gill realized he had misunderstood her, thinking back to the time they had gone to the pub soon after her arrival in Shelmouth.

★ ★ ★

Later, full of food and feeling as content as a sleepy kitten, she tried hard to remember why she had come to see Pete. Knowledge was accompanied by a return of apprehension. The envelope of share certificates — there it was, carelessly thrown aside and in danger of being forgotten. Reality suddenly crowded in. The boatyard, Graham, the painting . . .

She stared over the rim of her coffee-mug.

'Can we be serious, Pete? We've got to talk.'

His face mirrored hers as the smile faded, and he leaned back in his chair as if consciously trying to distance himself from her. One eyebrow flew up in familiar mockery.

'Something about a proposition, wasn't it? Sounds good!'

The forgotten fire glowed bravely, even as it died, and the tight silence stretching between them seemed out of place. Gill cleared her throat and summoned all her resources of strength.

'I want that painting back, Pete. And in return I'm giving you these.' She handed over the envelope and avoided his abrupt frown.

Time appeared to stand still as she watched him rip open the large packet and take out the contents. She was tense with foreboding. Suppose he refused to accept her gift? Supposing he wouldn't return the painting? Suppose, suppose . . .

'I see,' he said casually.

With a feeling of almost comic anticlimax, Gill watched his long fingers sort through the share certificates. Having half expected him to tear the lot into bits, or even throw them back at her, she was unnerved by this enigmatic behaviour.

Carefully he examined the change of ownership registered on each one and then paid the same meticulous attention to the deed of gift. And then, when she thought she could bear the silence no longer, he looked at her as he shuffled the pile of documents together before slowly returning them to the envelope.

Gill tensed. This was the moment she was dreading.

'You must want that picture very badly,' Pete remarked. 'I wonder why? I didn't realize Graham meant so much to you: does he?'

'He's my cousin,' she defended flatly. Suddenly, the deeper innuendo stung her into hasty denial. 'Good heavens, you must be joking! Graham actually isn't my type — and, anyways, he's got Brigitte. Good luck to them both, I say.'

Pete stretched his long legs and looked reflective.

'So just what *is* your type? Tell me. I'm interested.'

Colour rushed up her throat and stained her pale cheeks. Quickly she looked away from his searching eyes.

'I've met all sorts. But either they've been too ambitious, or too chauvinistic, or too — '

'Too what?'

She pulled fraying edges of self-control together with a last spurt of endurance and stared back defiantly. 'Too interested in other women!'

'Hmm. I wondered if being too old a friend ever came into it — '

For a long moment they looked at each other and Gill's confusion grew. What did he mean? What could he mean? Was he referring to their adolescence, when childish companionship had temporarily deepened into wilder feelings, ending inevitably in first kisses and passionate goodbyes, none of them destined to last?

Deep inside her, something stirred and the old pain reared. Surely he couldn't mean what she so longed to hear? Of course not. He was going to marry Lindsey.

In a voice sharp with anguish, she said quickly. 'No, nothing like that. I've always considered the past to be over — no strings attached to anything. Or anyone . . . we have to live in the present. Don't you agree, Pete?'

He blinked and seemed to be surfacing from thoughts of something far away.

'Oh, absolutely. The present. Yes, that's all that matters.'

With relief rushing through her, she watched him get out to the kitchen. She heard the kettle being filled.

'More coffee?' he called, and she snatched at the opportunity the question offered.

'No, thanks. I must be getting back,

it's late. So — if I could take the painting with me, please . . . '

No sound until Pete reappeared several minutes later, steaming mug in hand, and a blank expression on his face which made her thudding heart beat all the faster. How well she knew that look: it meant he had gone to earth, was refusing to make a decision, wouldn't commit himself to anything.

'Still here?' He sounded sardonic. 'Ah — you're waiting for the painting. Of course. Sorry I've kept you hanging about for so long. Didn't realize at first that the picture was the prime reason for you being here. Sorry, Gill.'

He took the small package from inside his father's locked roll-top desk and handed it to her. 'Silly, but I had the daft idea that you came just to see me. Well, we live and learn, don't we?'

She picked up her bag, slung her anorak over one shoulder, shrinking from the coldness of his words, the icy chips in his eyes, and edged towards the door. But his voice followed relentlessly as she stepped out into the night.

'Thanks for the shares, by the way. A fair exchange, I suppose, that painting being so important to you. I never thought you'd stay at the yard, you know — not really your cup of tea, neither the place nor the people . . . Well, if I don't see you again before you leave, cheers, Gill, and good luck.'

Aghast, she watched the door slam shut, leaving her alone, trembling, and full of a shocking sense of disbelief. She hadn't known Pete could be so cruel.

Slowly, with the wind slapping in from the sea and a fine rain beginning to sting her ashen face, she found the car and drove home. It was a very long time before she slept that night.

* * *

In the morning she threw herself into work to escape the recurring memories of the previous evening. But it wasn't finished yet.

Just as she was drinking her coffee, the door opened and Pete came in.

He put a large, familiar, envelope on her desk and said flatly, 'Sorry about last night, Gill. Let my feelings get the better of me, I'm afraid.'

The barest smile hovered over his set mouth and then died. 'Not as invulnerable to emotions as you are, obviously.'

Gill made a sound to protest, but he went on as if he hadn't heard her.

'Well, I've had time to think it all over now and, of course, I can't possibly take the shares. I don't want them — your grandfather meant you to have them and that's an end to it. And the picture is Graham's, no matter how he got hold of it. It's up to him what he does with it now.'

Abruptly, he leaned forward, hands on the far edge of her desk, staring at her with hard, darkly-pupilled eyes.

'And because you and I have always

been fond of each other — a long time ago — I claim the right to give you a last word of advice. Oh, yes, I know . . . no strings and all that. But I'm going to have my say. Don't get involved, Gill. Please. Just — don't get involved . . . '

They stared at each other in silence and her mind raced with bewilderment.

'Pete,' she whispered, but he had stepped away and was in the doorway.

'I must get back to work. I've found the blueprints of that new keel Graham insisted on using in both the *Melinda*'s and I've pin-pointed the weakness. It's just as I thought — he was too pig-headed to listen when we were building, but now he'll have to admit the whole mess is his fault.'

He looked back over his shoulder and Gill's heart sank as she recognized the grim expression of triumph on his face. So there would be an almighty confrontation as soon as Graham and he met up again. Without further thought, she blurted out:

'Couldn't you — wouldn't it be better not to tell him? Not at once? I mean, surely you could wait until he's dealt with his personal problems . . . '

Pete's old, hard look seared her. 'It's time we had things out,' he said tersely and slammed the door behind him.

Gill felt she could cope no more. Things had got beyond her control. She knew now, with a weary wryness, that Pete had been right when he told her not to become involved, but she was realizing the fact too late.

She was, after all, very deeply involved. She was the one who had discovered Graham's embezzlements, had impulsively given away her shares in the business and, worst of all, in some inexplicable way, she had alienated Pete from her. But what had she done, what had she said, to make him so forbidding and so completely unlike the kind, sensitive man she'd always known him to be?

It was no good. Her head ached and

her mind refused to concentrate. And she was shivering . . .

Just before lunch, Gill accepted the inevitable and left the office, asking the receptionist to deal with any phone calls, and went to bed for the rest of the day. Whether it was Aunt Mary's flu bug she'd caught or just a convenient collapse which would allow her to hide away for a few hours, she never found out. All she knew was that it was heaven to be relaxed and warm, in the safe privacy of her own quiet room, with all access to further trouble firmly denied.

★ ★ ★

After a long, refreshing sleep which lasted into early evening, she awoke feeling that an impossible burden had fallen from her shoulders. She felt strong enough to put on her dressing-gown and go downstairs in search of food and drink.

There was no sign of Lindsey, but

a note propped against the coffee-pot on the kitchen table caught Gill's eye at once.

Sorry you're not well. Pete said you'd left the office early and was worried about you. I looked in, but you were sleeping like a log, so I didn't wake you when I had my meal. See you tomorrow. Lindsey.

Gill read and reread the scribbled message and the old confusion returned again. How had Pete known she'd left the office? Had he been looking for her? Was he really worried? Certainly, last night he'd seemed concerned about her — but, no, nothing made sense any more. He and Lindsey were out together now, as usual, and she was here, alone.

Halfway back to bed with a glass of milk and an apple, Gill recalled something strange. Lindsey was out every night, including yesterday evening — and yet Pete had been alone in his cottage when she called. What on earth was going on?

The headache had returned. Feebly, Gill gave up her efforts to work things out and slipped back into the warmth of her bed. Perhaps she would be more sensible tomorrow.

★ ★ ★

Melinda II limped safely into harbour during the morning and Gill, watching at the interior window, saw how all the men in the yard downed tools at once, hurrying to the slipway to help moor the damaged craft and welcome Neil as he came ashore, looking disconsolate and upset.

Pete's tall figure was like a magnet, drawing a cluster of men and boys around him as he stood discussing the boat's problems with the returning skipper. Gill stepped back from the window quickly as the group broke up, for fear Pete should see her. She didn't feel ready for another confrontation. But just before lunch she was startled by his entrance into the office.

'So you're back? Feel better? You still look pale . . . '

His obvious but unexpected concern made her dither and then say, in an unnecessarily snappish voice, 'Don't keep going on about how awful I look, please. Yes, I'm fine again now.' And then she wished she could recall the words when she saw his face change and become stiffly expressionless.

'OK. I get the message. I'll leave you in peace, if that's what you want. Guess I should know by now, anyway . . . '

He stalked off towards the door and then, just as she hurriedly left her desk, knowing that somehow she must apologize for being so rude, there was a commotion in the passage outside.

She heard Pete saying, 'So you're back earlier than you said; and about time, too. There's a lot of problems to be sorted out here.'

Pete returned to the office, deliberately ignoring Gill, and crossed the room to stand with his back to the window that looked out onto the harbour.

'Well, let's clear the air a bit, shall we, Graham?'

Gill watched her cousin enter, his colour high and an uneasy expression narrowing his eyes. He stepped past her blindly, staring at Pete as he did so.

'This is all I need, *Melinda* in trouble, coming home without Brigitte, and then a greeting like this. For God's sake, Pete, back off a bit, can't you? I need a drink and something to eat — the trip was rough and I had no breakfast . . . '

Gill felt a shiver run through her and wildly sought a reason to leave the room. There was an atmosphere of potential danger already in the air; she realized Pete was ready to force Graham to his knees and didn't relish being a witness to such humiliation. Her hand reached out, feeling the edge of the open door. But there was to be no escape. Both men turned their heads, abruptly acknowledging her presence.

Pete's voice was icy: 'No. Stay here,

Gill,' and Graham repeated uneasily. 'Don't go,' as if he hoped that if she stayed she might deflect some of Pete's obvious anger.

Grudgingly, and with a feeling of dismay, she closed the door, knowing that all decision had been taken from her. They both needed her here, so she must stay.

Returning to her desk, she sat down quietly, as tense as a coiled spring, waiting for the next move.

Pete leaped to the attack hungrily.

'Two matters for your immediate attention, Graham, and both of them serious. We'll take *Melinda* first.'

'It's that MacDowall engine that's the trouble — I told you it was rubbish, but you wouldn't listen . . . ' Graham was blustering, but Gill knew from the loudness of his voice that he was simply trying it on.

Pete interrupted.

'It's not the engine at all, and well you know it, Graham. You aren't much of a sailor, but at least you know the difference between engine trouble and a basic fault in construction — which is what the real trouble is. It's that newfangled keel you designed, the one that sank the prototype, *Melinda I*, and *killed* my father.'

Graham's face had gone an ugly grey colour. As Gill watched fascinated yet repelled, she saw a slow flush of mottled purple riding up his fleshy cheeks. Then he was out of his chair, thumping the table and almost shrieking his instant denial.

'What a load of nonsense! That's all you can think about, isn't it, the accident with *Melinda*? You come back to it again and again, like a dog with a bone — always looking for some nasty little hiccup so that you can fix the blame on me. Well, for the last time, I didn't kill your father — and if you ever mention the matter again. I'll — I'll . . . '

'Yes?' Pete said lazily. 'Tell me, Graham, what will you do?' He was quiet, almost relaxed, and Gill realized, with a shock of horror, that he had achieved what he set out to do — to arouse Graham to an increasingly uncontrollable fury.

Urgently, and without thinking further, she said sharply, 'Stop it, Pete! Rows won't resolve *Melinda*'s trouble. All this is leading nowhere.'

'Oh, yes it is. Just look at the state poor old Graham's in.'

Pete laughed a cold, brief sound with no amusement in it, and Gill's mind opened. Of course! Why hadn't she realized it before? Pete was forcing Graham into that state of neurotic hysteria which she'd suspected he was prone to on a couple of previous occasions.

Facts jumped, abruptly fitting into the unfinished jigsaw. This was what Aunt Mary had been anxious about — Graham's uncontrolled outbursts. And Pete was still goading him on.

'Anyone listening right now wouldn't have much faith in you as designer and managing director of Wayland's

Boatyard, Graham. Don't you think it's time you gave it all up?'

'Get out of here this instant,' Graham yelled, leaving the desk and charging across the room, arms flailing. Pete put out one hand to hold him off and Gill quailed at the expression on his face, contemptuous and grim, it was the face of a stranger.

She could stand it no longer. In a trice she was at Graham's side, pulling him away, leading him back to his desk. She stared at Pete and heard her voice utter cold, authoritative words.

'Will you go, please? You've only made things worse. I'll deal with everything from now on. Graham and I don't need you any more, Pete.'

Even Graham's babbling curses ceased at that, and Gill and Pete stared at each other in stony silence. She was furious, and glad to be so. At last she could put aside her ridiculous feelings for him. He was vindictive and cruel and, thank goodness, she knew now just where she stood — on poor old

Graham's side. Her gaze didn't falter, as at last Pete broke the silence.

'I see.' His favourite answer when the chips were down, she recalled, and saw a sudden change of mood slide across his face. Anger died, and for a second she thought he looked distressed — hurt, even. And then she watched the return of the old, impersonal mask that was the customary defence of his secret vulnerability.

He moved quickly, passing her and making for the door. There he stopped and, without looking back, said quietly, 'I'm sorry, Gill, love,' and was gone. The door remained open and both Gill and Graham listened to his footsteps retreating down the long passage.

★ ★ ★

Gill looked at her cousin. She felt as if she had been engaged in a free-for-all wrestling bout — and had lost. But, despite her shock and pain, she clung to the fact that Graham needed help, which she was capable of giving him.

Watching him slump in the chair, hiding his face in his hands, she felt pity fill her. Remembering that he usually kept whisky in the office, she went to the cupboard and poured them both a stiff dram.

Then, putting his on the desk in front of him, she seated herself opposite and said, gently but firmly. 'Drink up, Graham. You'll feel better in a minute. Yes, go on, do as I say, and don't argue.'

Slowly, he lifted his head, and she saw how drawn his face had become, how his eyes were glassy and inward-looking, and her compassion grew. It was so obvious — why hadn't she seen the truth before? Clearly, her cousin was on the verge of a breakdown.

Leaning forward, she said quietly, 'I can help if you'll let me, please let me . . .'

She watched his eyes reluctantly focus on her, saw how his shaking hand clumsily groped for the glass, heard him gulping down the whisky, and then waited patiently until his mottled colour faded and he sat back in his chair, misery staring out of his crumpled face.

'No one can help,' he mumbled, avoiding her eyes. 'It's all gone too far. I've got myself in a terrible muddle and, of course, Pete was right, I'm not cut out to be a designer — or a businessman. I've always known it, but something made me go on and on.

'I suppose it was to prove to Dad that I was of some use after all. And now you've found out about the money, have you? You've seen the accounts? Looked in the safe? Oh, God, what a fool I've been.'

'Yes,' Gill agreed crisply. 'You certainly have, Graham. But don't give up hope. I'm on your side. And I know how you can sort out the financial side of things. Look, have another drink and listen to my plan.'

★ ★ ★

Thirty minutes later, Gill was smiling and Graham's face had taken on a more relaxed expression.

'We're not out of the woods yet,' she cautioned him, tidying away accounts and books from the desk. 'But if you do as I suggest, at least you'll square off all your debts. And then you must rethink about *Melinda* and the plans for the future.'

Graham rose, going to the window and looking out at the harbour, busy with small craft in the midday sunshine. His voice shook for a moment.

'You've been good, Gilly, I mean, after the way I treated you. I didn't want you here, you see.' Turning quickly, he looked back at her, and she saw his eyes were moist with unshed tears.

Gently, she said, 'I know. We never really hit it off as kids, did we? But things are different now, Graham. And I know all this muddle can be cleared up if you act quickly and take advice. Let's have some lunch, shall we? Come home with me, I'll make us a sandwich and some coffee.'

But as she left the room he remained by the window.

'Actually, I think I'll make a phone call first.'

She read his face correctly.

'Brigitte?'

Sheepishly, he returned her smile. 'Yes. Can't seem to manage without her, really.'

Returning to the desk, he lifted the receiver and looked at her again, anxiety in his eyes.

'Think she'll understand? Maybe she won't want to know any more — I mean, the mess I'm in with the money . . .'

'If she loves you, Graham, she'll stand by you.'

'Sure. Of course she will,' he said half-heartedly.

Gill left the room as he began to dial, and saw, with a feeling of relief, that he was smiling again.

When, later, he joined her for a snack

in the kitchen of The Lookout, he was almost the same old Graham, full of new-found strength, with a hint of familiar aggression evident in his loud voice and bustling manner.

'I'm driving up to London straight away,' he said confidently. 'Take the picture to Sotheby's before I meet Brigitte at Heathrow this evening. We'll stay in town overnight and come back tomorrow.'

His face clouded slightly, as he bit into a sandwich. 'Of course, there's bound to be more trouble with Pete about this *Melinda* business — but I'm sticking to my guns. He doesn't know what he's talking about, that keel is a winner. He's simply trying to put one over on me. I tell you what, Gill, I wouldn't put it past Pete that he's trying to get me out of the business . . . '

'Nonsense,' Gill declared firmly. But the idea wasn't as fanciful as it seemed at first. Pete had certainly talked about Graham getting his 'comeuppance'.

Was a resignation from the board really Pete's long-term goal?

Briskly, Gill made coffee and saw Graham off afterwards. She tried to keep an open mind as she returned to work. Things were still in a state of flux, but it was too much to hope that Graham would change completely from the power-motivated aggressor she'd known during the last few months. At least he was doing the sensible thing in settling his debts.

Then Pete's low voice came into her mind with hurtful clarity. They'd laughed together once, but she knew they would never be as close as that again. Not after the way she had ordered him out of the office this morning.

'*Graham and I don't need you any more.*' The autocratic words haunted her all afternoon, and it was with a feeling of relief that, as she locked the office behind her, she remembered that this was the night of Lindsey's birthday party. There was still a lot to do and, among the gaiety and bustle of the evening, at least she would be able to forget her own wretchedness.

★ ★ ★

As she headed for the kitchen to see how far final preparations had gone, Gill allowed herself one last moment of indulgent self-pity — Lindsey had Pete, and Graham had Brigitte. But she was alone; no one loved her. The thought stirred her into positive decision. It was time to go. She drew in a deep breath. Yes, once Graham had settled his financial affairs and found a girl to take her place in the office, she would pack up and return to London.

Doubtless, Lindsey would soon be marrying Pete and moving out of The Lookout — the house could then be rented for the summer. These few months she'd spent at Shelmouth would be behind her, with their bittersweet memories ... pain swept back, unexpectedly sharp and cloying, but resolutely she opened the kitchen door and at once was faced with the need for a change of mood.

'Thank goodness you're here!' Lindsey wailed, her pink face only just visible behind a battery of pans, dishes, and wonderful-looking food. 'I've only just finished the vol-au-vents, and now I'm running short of prawns — oh, Gill, what shall I do.'

'Leave it to me. I'll do something very clever with mushrooms instead, while you go up and make yourself beautiful!' Suddenly, it was good to be able to swing into action, doing something different, and stepping into a new, positive mood.

Gill snatched up her apron and looked over the littered table at Lindsey. 'Happy birthday,' she said warmly. 'You left before me this morning, so I couldn't say it then — and I'll bring your present down later. Have a wonderful evening.'

Lindsey paused in the doorway. Her

flushed face was wreathed in a beatific smile and the smudge of flour on one cheek only enhanced her youthful prettiness.

'Oh, I will! And thanks, Gill, for all your help. I'm going to miss you, you know, when I leave here.'

Turning away, Gill began to slice the mushrooms efficiently.

'Well, that's a nice thought, but I don't believe you! Engaged ladies only have one thing in mind, don't they? And I'm told marriage takes a whole lot of organizing! Now, hurry up and get ready — good heavens!' She glanced at her watch. 'Only another three-quarters of an hour and then they'll all be here. Up you go!'

It was a mad scramble to get everything set out on the shining oak table in the big drawing-room before the guests arrived. But with her usual rapid competence, Gill surveyed the flower-decked room before dashing up to change, well within the time limit, knowing that everything looked welcoming, with an abundance of attractive food and a good supply of drinks.

She switched on a tape, dimmed the lights, and went upstairs with the murmur of romantic music following her.

As the first guests arrived, their voices bringing new life and warmth to the old house, she gave a last look into her mirror before going down to join the party.

She looked elegant, but not eye-catching, she decided; it was Lindsey's night, and she knew she would make a good foil for the younger girl's brightness by wearing a plain dress, decorated only by a beautiful Mexican turquoise brooch at her throat.

She went downstairs quietly, ready to give Lindsey the party of her life, but knowing as she went that seeing Pete and Lindsey together was bound to be nerve-racking and hurtful. Despite her own feelings, though, she must put a good face on the situation.

But she was completely unprepared for the moment of truth, when it came, minutes later.

The drawing-room was already crowded with young people. Gill saw a gleam of colourful dresses and shining hair as she headed for the kitchen to bring through the last trays of food still hot from the oven.

Voices and music mingled in a hum of excitement and she smiled to herself as she opened the kitchen door — how lovely to be carefree and happy, she thought wistfully — and then her smile was switched off, for two figures were caught up in a deep embrace just inches away from her.

Lindsey and — but, no, it wasn't Pete whose arms held her so closely and possessively. Gill's involuntary gasp of amazement made the lovers jump apart, and she found herself staring into the equally surprised face of young Ian Robinson.

'You might've knocked!' he said,

grinning cheekily.

Gill was dumbfounded. She had been so sure it was Pete who loved Lindsey — but Lindsey was laughing at her from within Ian's arms, and quickly she must pull her bewildered thoughts together.

'Don't look so shocked, Gill — after all we are getting engaged tonight; and we've been going out for nearly six months now!'

'Six months?' Gill was trying hard to understand this startling new development.

Lindsey nestled closer to Ian.

'Mmm. Course, we had to keep it quiet — my dad and Ian's uncle have a long-standing family feud, and that's why it was wonderful to move in here with you. It meant I could go off and meet Ian without Mum always being suspicious of where I was. Oh, well, they've got used to the idea at last, and actually Mum thinks Ian is quite marvellous!'

Ian winked at Gill. 'I go and meet

her when she's bringing the shopping home, see? Useful things, taxi's . . . '

Lindsey slapped him playfully. 'Oh, you're wicked . . . '

The front doorbell rang and she grasped him firmly by the hand. 'That's probably Mum and Dad now — come on, love, let's go and meet them.'

Alone, Gill discovered her head was swimming. She caught hold of the nearby worktop to steady herself, and was just beginning to feel capable of returning to the party when above the hubbub of voices outside, she heard a footstep in the doorway, and looked back quickly.

Pete stood there, a tall, handsome, grey-suited Pete, whom she hardly recognized, except for the warmth in his vivid eyes as he said quietly. 'Thought I'd find you here, hiding away.' He came closer, deliberately looking her up and down and then nodding, as if in pleasure. 'You look stunning, love . . . '

Gill opened her mouth, but had no

words to answer. She heard him say something that made her head spin, and her heart began to thunder.

'There's something I want to ask you, Gill, something very important — '

8

Pete's question hung in the air, and Gill said weakly, at last, 'What — what is it you want to ask me?' She watched a grin spread across his face.

'Hang on. Put those plates down before you drop them. I don't want to be responsible for ruining Lindsey's party — that's it. And the other one . . . '

Bemused, she returned the food to the table, her eyes unable to leave his.

'Well?' Her throat was dry and the word sounded unfamiliarly high and brittle as one thought after another rushed through her mind.

A question, he'd said. Something important. And he was smiling down at her, his eyes gentle and almost pleading, in unmistakable eagerness. Was it possible that he was actually going to say he loved her? Was he going

278

to ask the one vital and wonderful question she had never thought to hear? Gill's heart raced in anticipation.

Pete's hands found hers, holding them, warm and secure. He smiled into her wide eyes and she thought she would die from an abundance of happiness; until he began to speak.

'It's a favour, actually, love. I want you to use your influence with Graham to persuade him to stop using that useless keel he put in *Melinda* on any future orders.'

Her head spun, and she wondered if she was hearing right. For this was no declaration of love, simply a plea for help to bring Graham even lower than he was at the moment. It was revenge, and not love.

Overwhelming disappointment mingled with a spurt of anger, and she jerked her hands away from him, her face and body trembling. But, in spite of the flooding emotions, one thing alone was going through her mind, helping her not to give way. He should never know how close she had been to throwing her arms around him, her lips so ready to meet his. Strength grew. Pete should never see her for the fool she undoubtedly was.

So, with tremendous self-control, she turned again to the plates of food, picked them up and headed for the sitting-room, managing to call over her shoulder, in a voice commendably matter-of-fact, 'I'll be back in a minute. I don't want these to get cold.'

By the time she returned to the kitchen, she was in full command of herself once more. Neither by look nor voice did she show those foolish feelings, so firmly stifled. 'Now, Pete — about that keel — '

A little flurry of inner amusement rose within her, as she walked towards the worktop and casually began clearing up. Funny, to talk about Graham's wretchedly inefficient keel when only minutes before she'd pictured talking, instead, about love and marriage.

Well, quite obviously he didn't love

her. Goodbye, marriage. And, yes, back to Graham — 'What is it exactly you want me to tell him, then?'

Pete was idly wandering about the kitchen, no longer smiling, she noted, but deeply concentrated and frowning. He came to a halt beside her as she threw scraps of pastry into the bin and piled dishes onto the draining-board.

'That he's got to delete his keel from the blueprints we use and substitute the one I wanted to put in originally. One your uncle approved of, one that's tried and tested. And I want an undertaking — in writing — from Graham that he won't do any more so called designing.'

The words tailed off as Gill looked up, meeting his eyes, unable suddenly to mask her feelings. 'You want an undertaking, Pete?' She made no attempt to keep the disapproving coolness out of her voice.

'I think you've forgotten that you're only a minority shareholder, after all; don't you mean 'we' want it? In future I'd like us to discuss plans together before you start dictating terms like this.'

Cold pleasure glowed through her. Just as well to let him know she wasn't merely a romantic, but a professional businesswoman as well. They stared at each other until Pete nodded, somewhat grudgingly.

'You're quite right,' he conceded. 'I should have asked your opinion first.' She knew what the admission must have cost him and some of her hurt pride began to heal. 'But, Gill, you must see why we have to do this? Graham's gone far enough with wrecking Wayland's past reputation. It must never happen again.'

Now he was looking at her with new respect — as if they were truly equals, Gill thought, placated. And this was how it must be from now on — equal working partners, and nothing more.

Briskly, she dried her hands, before turning away. 'Very well. I'll talk to Graham first thing tomorrow. And now

I'm going to join the party and enjoy myself . . . '

But in the doorway, she couldn't stop herself pausing to glance back at him, still standing there, watching her with unfathomable eyes. 'Coming?' she asked in a gentler voice and was glad to see a hint of the old sardonic humour lift his sombre face.

'Thought you'd never ask — '

* * *

Together they went into the noisy, thronged, sitting-room. From then on, Gill found it easier to keep her deep-rooted pain at bay. She must play it all very cool, be wary with Pete, continue working with him, yet never allowing herself to put a step out of place to endanger this new, frail relationship.

The evening had already provided several shocks, the most important being that he didn't, after all, love Lindsey. But that romantic dream of a happy ending only minutes ago still clouded her mind and Gill knew she was no nearer a resolution to her emotional problems than she had been earlier.

And there was still a lot to be done, businesswise. Well, she would play her part with as great a competence as she possessed, and never again let herself slip into foolish sentiment.

So she allowed the party spirit to draw her into its warmth and noise, and actually managed to enjoy the rest of the evening. And, by the time a few drinks had relaxed her, she was able to regard Lindsey's unmistakable happiness with affection and no hint of envy.

For it was wonderful to see life working out so well for two such attractive and likeable young people. She wished them well and joined in the rowdy toast to 'Lindsey and Ian' with all her heart, as the evening drew to a close.

As she put down her glass, an arm went around her waist. Turning, she stared into Pete's smile.

'May I have the last dance?' One dark eyebrow was lifted in the old, mocking way, and she stepped into his arms without any constraint. She knew, now, exactly where she stood with him. So why not enjoy such moments as these, offered in simple friendship and accepted in the same, undemanding spirit?

The music was old-fashioned and smoochy, and someone had turned the lights out, leaving the glow from the hall to illuminate the shadowy room.

A few couples only remained now, silent and close, locked away from the boisterous farewells being shouted through the hall and open front doorway of the old house. Gill's cheek was warm against Pete's rough face. We dance well together, she thought, their bodies complementing each other, their steps following without hindrance.

When the tape ended they clung together for a moment longer, and it was Gill who finally moved away.

'That was nice,' she said mildly, and marvelled inwardly at her self-control. Pete's hand still held hers. He stood beside her, drawing her back to look at him again.

'Yes, very nice. We must do it more often. Gill — '

She waited for a long moment. 'Yes, Pete?'

His fingers came up, gently outlining her cheek, her mouth, her throat. 'Forgive me for all the times I've been nasty.'

It wasn't what she'd expected him to say. She laughed breathlessly, her eyes suddenly swimming with lost love, thankful for the darkness that hid them. 'Of course; only one condition.'

'Anything.'

'That you forgive me, too?'

'Ah, but you're never nasty, are you? Aloof, arrogant at times, cross, often, extremely stupid, but not nasty . . . '

They were laughing and the intimate moment was over. She led him into the well-lit hall.

'Compliments will get you nowhere! Now go home, Pete, I need all the beauty sleep I can get if I have to beard Graham in his den tomorrow — '

'G'night, love.' Again his arms were around her, and briefly he drew her towards him. Coolly, Gill stepped away.

'Goodnight, Pete.'

★ ★ ★

She helped a dreamy-eyed Lindsey make attempts to clear up the remnants of the party, but once the remaining food and drink had been put away they looked at each other, yawned, and agreed to leave the rest.

'I'll be up early,' Lindsey promised, already on her way upstairs.

'Don't worry. There's always tomorrow. And the next day.'

Gill switched off all the lights and followed her up, thinking as she did so that what she had just said was a good maxim for her future life. One day at a time . . .

As she undressed and slipped into bed, suddenly inexpressibly weary, she reflected on the evening's events. A happy ending for Lindsey and Ian's romance. And what of hers? Not exactly a happy ending but not a disastrous ending, either. For Pete was unattached, after all, and once he had been fond of her . . .

Gill shut her eyes and allowed herself a last, delicious hope that maybe he might grow fond of her again. But she must go slow, be careful, not showing her own feelings —

Thought ceased, and she slept.

★ ★ ★

In the harsh morning light, with the sound of a menacing ground-swell sucking at the harbour walls, she dressed slowly, consciously turning her thoughts inwards to sort out the order of her day. A tiny thread of hopeful happiness had entered her life since last night — something new she could cling to, without allowing it to overwhelm her self-control.

It was a good feeling, a spark of warmth lighting up the cloudy future which she intuitively sensed lay ahead, preparing her for whatever problems might come her way.

And problems there were, without doubt. Almost as soon as she had opened the day's post and made a couple of phone calls, voices sounded in the passage outside the office and then Graham strode in, his face a dark cloud of resentment.

Pete followed, ignoring Gill and standing by the desk in an almost threatening attitude as Graham angrily slumped into the big chair opposite.

They carried on their conversation as if they were alone and Gill watched and listened, realizing at once that neither man was willing to back down in this particular hostile confrontation.

Graham, as usual; sought refuge in blustering generalities.

'Trust you to pick on me about this!

It's all you can think of, always blaming me for whatever happens — '

Pete's voice was low but incisive; with compassion for her cousin growing, Gill realized that Pete's controlled anger and logical reasoning must win.

'Let's forget personalities, Graham. The facts are what matter. And the fact is that the problems of both *Melinda*'s stem from your inadequate design. We've had her up on the blocks and it's plain where the trouble lies.'

'There's only your word for that! Who do you think you are? A naval architect? I tell you — '

Graham started his old trick of thumping the table, but Pete's continued coolness effectively reduced him to sullen silence.

'No, let me tell you, Graham: I had Arthur Conway over from Torquay yesterday afternoon — '

'Huh! I thought he died years ago. He should be dead — used to design our boats over fifty years ago.'

'Exactly. Just the point I was leading up to. Thanks for making it so plain.'

They glared across the desk. Then slowly Pete relaxed, pushing hands into his trouser pockets and briefly smiling down at his discomforted adversary. Quietly, he continued.

'Fifty years ago, Graham, this yard had no equal in the West Country, because of its reputation for seaworthy craft, and that reputation lasted for nearly half a century; until you decided to make changes.'

Graham's bluster had left him. He scowled down at the Victorian inkwell in front of him and played mindlessly with his pen.

'Progress doesn't allow things to stand still, I'll have you know.'

'Progress?' There was so much contempt in that one word that Gill felt sorrier still for her cousin. Without doubt Pete was enjoying the humiliation he was forcing on Graham. She remembered his stern, secret expression which she had found so fearsome, and knew now, with dismay, that Pete's hour of victory had come, and he had every intention of making the most of it.

Relentlessly, she broke in, forcing both men to suddenly look at her.

'May I suggest we cut short this very unpleasant argument and get on with business, rather than indulging further in personal qualities?'

She felt Pete's instant frown, but ignored it, continuing smoothly, 'Forgive me if I act as mediator, but it seems necessary. Graham — ' She looked hard at her cousin's bowed head, and slowly he met her eyes. He appeared stricken, all his anger gone, replaced now by a bleakness which struck deep into her.

'Graham,' she said in a more kindly tone, 'Pete and I are asking you to abandon your keel design. As Pete has said, and Mr Conway has confirmed, the facts speak for themselves. Both the *Melindas* suffered damage because of inferior design. We have no alternative, therefore, but to go back to the old blueprints — the ones Uncle Harry and Dad used so successfully. So please agree, and then we need waste no more time with this stupid squabbling . . . '

She smiled forcefully at Graham, taking no notice of Pete's almost inaudible comment as he abruptly walked across the room to the window, turning his back and staring out at the harbour.

'Oh, very well. I'm fed up with this whole place — and everyone in it. It's old, it's ugly, it reeks of conniving and ambition, it . . . '

'And it keeps you in the lifestyle you enjoy.' There was no denying the scorn on Pete's voice, but Gill kept her smile steadily fixed as she nodded down at Graham.

'I agree,' she said, reassuringly. 'It may be all you say, but it still has terrific potential, and if you'll let Pete and I have a little more control, we can fulfil that potential. You're not a born businessman, Graham, let's admit it — your talent lies in more artistic directions.'

For a second Gill feared his fury might return, but, no, he was looking at her wonderingly, with a brightening of his sullen face.

'So give us the OK about the keel and then *Melinda*'s troubles can be cleared up. Monsieur Leconte isn't going to wait for ever, you know, and we need his cheque to pay the bills incurred . . . '

She waited, unsure if she'd gone too far. Pete would almost certainly resent her continued interference: Graham might well decide, after all, not to play along. She held her breath and felt the silence grow tense.

Surprisingly, it was Pete who broke it. Leaving the window, he came across to her, putting a hand briefly on her shoulder, before staring down at Graham. 'Gill has put it very neatly, all in a nutshell. Wayland's Yard is what matters, Graham. So let's have your answer, then — '

Wearily, Graham stretched back in his imposing chair. He searched first Pete's eyes, then Gill's.

'Do what you want,' he said at last. 'I'm no match for either of you high-powered, ambitious business types. All I want is peace and quiet and my pictures. And Brigitte.' The mere mention of her name brought a swift smile and he looked suddenly happier, as he added, 'I think I'll phone her right now.'

Pete's face showed no elation. He caught Gill's eye, nodded, and then looked back at Graham.

'Thanks,' he said flatly. 'And just one more thing — I intend to take *Melinda* on trials myself, once the repairs are made, and I want you to be there to see the difference. OK?'

'To rub my nose in it? Oh, yes — yes, if I must.' Graham was already dialling and Gill followed Pete to the office door, expecting him to make some comment.

But Pete went rapidly down the

passage without looking back, and she closed the door, behind her to give Graham privacy for his call to Brigitte, feeling as if she, like Graham, had been trodden underfoot by a man whose only feelings were of revenge and ambition.

* * *

She paced the empty corridor, her mind occupied. She knew now that her personal plans, whatever they were, must be shelved until such time as the boatyard had overcome this difficult period and got back on its feet again. If Pete and she were to run the business without Graham, the responsibility such a decision entailed must be of prime importance.

And she knew, too, with a feeling of apprehension, that sharing the responsibility with Pete was bound to be demanding. For admiring Pete's business skills as she did, she loved him as well. And love wasn't the easiest of emotions to handle in such a working relationship.

Her thoughts were steady and realistic. She would do the best she could. But one other thing hovered in her mind. Pete's relentless hounding of Graham was unpleasant, and she had the feeling it wasn't over yet. There were still storm clouds on the horizon.

* * *

It was a relief, later that afternoon, to lock the office behind her and go and visit Aunt Mary, whose welcoming smile and healthy appearance was an immediate comfort.

'You look so much better — how do you feel?' Gill asked, kissing her aunt and then following her into the kitchen, where the kettle sang and a plate of freshly-baked scones stood beside bowls of clotted cream and home-made strawberry jam.

'Quite different, my dear. Haven't felt so well for months. But I can't say the same for you — you look strained and much too thin. Now sit down, dear, do, and have some of that cream. You need fattening up, my girl!'

Gill laughed and felt the cares of recent weeks subside a little.

'If you had your way, Aunt Mary, I'd be a walking testimony to your good home-cooking, I know.' She glanced at her aunt as she brewed the tea, wondering how much to say about the problems of the new boat, and whether to hint that Graham was in trouble.

The older woman sat down placidly and poured tea into eggshell-thin china cups. She passed one to Gill, pushed the cream nearer, and said quietly, 'You've had a hard time since you came home, Gill. Oh, yes, I know . . . ' Her lined face smiled a little ruefully. 'Village gossip never lets up. So even although you've tried to spare me, I know what's been going on.'

Anxiously, Gill frowned. But Aunt Mary's face was serene again as she sipped her tea. 'Life's full of problems,' she mused sagely. 'And we bring them on ourselves, usually. Graham, now — always trying to do what he wasn't cut out for. I'm thankful that Miss Leconte's such a nice, sensible girl. She loves him, and she'll look after him, I'm sure.'

Gill looked at her jam-piled plate. She might have known that Graham's unpredictable life was public property. Then her face fell.

'What else have you heard, Aunt Mary?'

'That you and Pete keep falling out . . . ' The answer was swift and to the point. Aunt Mary's eyes flashed and Gill felt a small child again, being told off by this kindest, yet most realistic of aunts.

'How can you both be so foolish?' she demanded sternly. 'You're made for each other! So why must you waste time like this? Life doesn't stand still, you know!'

Gill was bewildered. 'Well, I — I — ' Slowly she pulled herself together.

'I think Pete has something on his mind,' she confided at last and met Aunt Mary's eyes across the table.

'Until that's settled, you've just got to sit and wait, Gill. Pete's an awkward customer, I know. And he'll know no peace until he's achieved what he's set out to do . . .'

Aunt Mary's smile flashed out. 'Men!' she exploded and then changed the subject. 'Some more tea, my dear?'

★ ★ ★

When Gill returned home, she found Lindsey and Ian both busily clearing up the last traces of the previous night's celebrations. Lindsey switched off the vacuum and Ian stopped rearranging the furniture, turning to look at Gill with smiling faces.

'So there you are!' Lindsey burst out impetuously. 'Gill, we want to thank you for such a super time yesterday — it was really great of you to let us have the party here. I do hope there wasn't too much mess — and no damage?'

'If there was, I'm sure you've dealt with it! No, don't worry, Lindsey, it was a terrific pleasure to be able to share in your happiness. Don't bother with it any more, I've got the whole evening in front of me . . . off you go, make the most of your brand-new engagement!'

She watched them exchange smiles and suddenly experienced a terrible moment of personal truth, bleakly knowing that while Pete still harboured his relentless longing to show Graham up, there could be no such close union between her and Pete. For he was a man apart, motivated by hatred, and therefore untouched by love, fond of her as he occasionally seemed to be.

Coldness swept through Gill and, alone again in the silent house, she felt a return to despair and frustration. But no longer did she allow it to direct her life; it was merely a shadow to be lived with and endured. For ever, if necessary.

That philosophy helped her through the following days, immersing herself in work, of which there was an increasing amount. Despite the inevitable publicity about *Melinda II*, inquiries kept coming in, and by the end of the week Gill had successfully negotiated the initial clauses of a contract to build a similar luxury cruiser.

* * *

Heady with self-approval, she threw an impulsively warm smile at Pete when he came into the office on a sunlit April morning, his unexpected appearance making her day that much brighter and happier.

'Commander and Mrs Bronson are coming in on Thursday afternoon to have a last talk with you before signing,' she said gaily, and basked in the look he gave her, seeing warmth softening the blue of his eyes and lifting the set firmness of his mouth.

'Clever girl,' he said softly. 'Go on like this and we'll all be millionaires, just like Graham!'

They laughed together, then Gill's face straightened.

'Poor old Graham — will he always be the butt of silly, unkind jokes?' she asked wistfully. 'I do hope not, Pete — he's trying so hard to get himself sorted out again. And Brigitte's backing him magnificently. I honestly think he's come to a turning-point in his life. Maybe now he'll find something that he can do well and really enjoy. Wouldn't that be wonderful?'

But, even as she spoke, she watched Pete's warmth retreat. He looked at her with a return of the familiarly frightening hardness.

'Miracles don't happen,' he told her shortly. 'And why should they? Graham still has a lot to answer for.'

Gill's world rocked uncertainly. She longed to tell Pete that by fostering his hatred for Graham he was diminishing himself, but she hadn't the nerve to do so. Instead, looking away from him, she said quietly, 'He also has to settle up for the Van Praken picture. His friend Erik will be here this evening for the money. I overheard them make arrangements . . . but I've no idea how Graham's going to manage to pay.'

Pete walked around the desk and sat down in Graham's large, managerial chair. He caught Gill's disapproving eye, grinned briefly, and got up again. 'It's not my style, thanks very much. If Graham goes — and I think he's got the message at last — I'll leave the paperwork to you and carry on doing what I've always done, supervising in the yard.

'And I shouldn't worry about the inscrutable Erik turning up. I've had a word with the harbour-master, and several of the local fishermen, and they're all watching out for him. I don't imagine he'll get far enough in to actually land again and start blackmailing poor dear Graham.'

'But the picture must be paid for, surely?' Gill was confused. Why should Pete try to help Graham like this? Or was it just another ruse to further his own ideas of revenge?

'Oh, yes. I believe Graham's selling another old master to raise the cash. Sad, isn't it?'

He smiled mercilessly, and Gill shivered. The hatred was still there. Would it never die? She returned to her work.

'I'm busy, Pete. So, unless you want something, may I get on?'

He seemed unruffled by her sharpness, pausing by her chair before heading for the door.

'Just one thing more. I'm taking *Melinda II* out on trials tomorrow morning. I'd like you to come.'

Wonderingly, she raised her head to meet his eyes.

'Please,' he added, and his smile was as sweet and warm as it had been in the days of their growing up.

'All right. If you really want me to — '

'I do.'

She nodded. 'Then I'll be there. Ten o'clock?'

'On the dot. Well done, love.'

As usual, he slammed the door behind him, and she was left grinning beatifically at the papers spread out before her. Would she never learn?

★ ★ ★

Brigitte Leconte came in to say hello during the afternoon, and something else as well.

'Gill, I must thank you for helping Graham. We both are so grateful for all you've done — and are still doing. He has accepted that he must leave this place, so once all the business of repaying the money is done, we shall go home to France.'

'To live?' Gill studied Brigitte's lovely face and saw a tender strength in the glowing smile that satisfied her.

'But yes, of course! I have a cousin whose château contains many fine pictures, as well as an uncatalogued library, Graham will work there, and we will be very happy.'

'I do hope so. He deserves to be happy for a change. And so do you, Brigitte. You've stood by him so wonderfully.'

Brigitte looked surprised, and her dark eyes softened. 'But naturally,' she said simply. 'You see, I love him.'

Gill bowed her head, and when she looked up again, the momentary stab of pain had passed, She smiled approvingly and changed the subject.

'And are you coming on *Melinda*'s sea trials tomorrow? Pete's asked Graham to go.'

Brigitte made a humorous little grimace. 'I have so much to do; the bank manager to see, my father to telephone . . . ' She rose and smiled mischievously down at Gill. 'So please look after my Graham for me; the forecast is bad, and he dislikes the sea, especially in bad weather.'

'Don't worry,' Gill answered in the same flippant vein. 'I'll have a lifebelt all ready in case of accidents!'

Laughing, Brigitte said goodbye, and Gill reflected on Graham's immense good fortune in having attracted the love and understanding of such a humane and beautiful woman. It seemed that his troubles were over now — a new, more congenial job, his financial affairs in order once more, and love offered, so freely given.

Gill forbade herself the indulgence of envying him, for the last few days had brought a new feeling of maturity, and she knew she had much to be thankful for herself.

She had a position of responsibility which brought with it the satisfaction of continuing the work carried out by her father and uncle. She had this comfortable home, a growing warm relationship with Aunt Mary; sufficient money for her needs and — she breathed a little more deeply — Pete at her side, as a colleague and friend. She must be grateful for all these blessings and not ever long for more. She must be content.

* * *

The brightness of the sunshine was blotted out by racing grey clouds and a suggestion of rain in the wind when she went to her bedroom window the next morning. Brigitte had been right about the bad forecast.

How unkind! A trip on *Melinda II* in calm waters would have been much more to her taste than dressing up in weatherproof gear and having to hang on for dear life as the waves lifted the craft in a succession of roller-coasting ups and downs.

At five-to-ten she went out into the yard, heading for the slipway where *Melinda II* was moored. She held the secret warmth of Pete's unexpected invitation close to her, and knew that however foul the weather, she would always remember this trip, as cementing their business relationship, as well as their friendship.

How right she was, for it was to prove totally unforgettable . . .

Pete and Graham, as if by mutual consent, took no notice of each other when they boarded *Melinda*. Gill went below at once, entering the stateroom with Graham behind her. Immediately he began to complain.

'What a day! Not my idea of seagoing weather — Pete's a fool to go out in this. He could just as easily have waited till tomorrow when it's calmed down.' He mooched over to the cocktail cabinet. 'Think I'll have a drink. What about you, Gill?'

'No thanks. And wouldn't it be better if you kept a clear head? After all, this isn't just a joyride, you know.'

Irritated by his stupidity, Gill spoke sharply, and then wished she'd held her tongue as Pete looked down the companionway, frowning when he saw Graham with a bottle in his hand.

'For God's sake! It's not a party, Graham — and I want you up here on deck. You won't get a true idea of how she's riding the weather if you stay down there drinking.'

Graham knocked back a whisky in one huge gulp, as if in bravado. He glared back at Pete with all the old signs of dislike and aggravation.

'We're not all miserable sobersides like you, Oakridge! Wouldn't do you any harm to have a drink yourself, loosen up a bit . . . OK?'

'Oh, all right. I want to keep an eye on you today.'

For five minutes or so Gill stayed below, uncertain of what to do. It was dry and comfortable down here and, as she could see through the streaming portholes, outside the weather was fast deteriorating. Rain hit the glass in slanting rods and a growing queasiness in her stomach made her realize the merciless force of the waves. And, as yet, *Melinda II* was still only in the estuary mouth. She dreaded the thought of the menacing ocean, just a few hundred yards away.

Then she recalled, from choppy sailing-trips with her father, that it was more comfortable to be in the open air when sickness threatened, however wet and fierce the conditions. So, firmly fastening her anorak and pulling up the hood, she left the stateroom, emerging on deck just as *Melinda* rounded the thin finger of the sandy point, to be met at once with a blast of wind that juddered through the craft.

Staggering a little, Gill grabbed the rail, and was nearly washed off her feet by an immense wave which hit the prow in a splendid cascade of blue-green, frothing water. Pete's voice came from behind her.

'Back here, Gill.' And blindly she made her way safely into the warmth of the cabin, where Pete, Graham and Neil Peters stood; tall, hooded figures in their colourful wet-weather gear, topped by orange life-jackets, balancing on the bucking deck as they manoeuvred the boat out towards the rain-lashed, hazy horizon.

★ ★ ★

The noise was deafening, wind and rain mingled in an ear-splitting cacophony that Gill found hard to get used to. But once her first alarm was over, she began to enjoy the experience. Truly, the sea was a terrifying monster . . . one glance at Graham's ashen face made her realize the fear it could engender. She nudged him.

'Are you all right?' she asked, in a shout that only just reached him, and he nodded impatiently.

'Of course I am!'

He turned away, watching the panel in front of him, listening with a frown to Pete's comments, and to Neil's answering advice. Then, unexpectedly, he rolled towards the open doorway.

Gill watched him reach the rail and cling to it, immersed in the next wave as it billowed over the boat. Her sympathy was deep, and she was about to go out and comfort him, when suddenly, there was a crash which ran through the boat from prow to stern.

When Gill recovered from the impact of the gigantic wave, she looked out, but saw no one. It took a long, terrifying moment to realize what had happened. She grabbed at Pete's arm.

'Graham's gone overboard!' she screamed. Pete shook off her hand without taking his eyes away from the instrument panel.

'The idiot! Trust him to do something stupid.'

'Pete!' The hysteria in her voice reached him at last, and he met her eyes, scowling. 'Do something,' she ordered savagely. 'He can't swim! We've got to help him.'

Another wave swamped the boat. Pete's eyes bored into Gill's, and he yelled over his shoulder to Neil Peters. 'Take over. Keep her as even as you can.'

Roughly, he pushed past Gill, grabbing

at a line as he did so, then bending to look down at the sucking, pounding waters that frothed around the boat.

'There! Over there . . . ' Gill saw Graham first, a heap of crumpled yellow plastic, borne up by the inflated orange life-jacket.

'Get back, Gill!' Swiftly Pete tied the nylon rope around his waist. 'You're not safe out here.'

'I'm not going.'

He glared over his shoulder, then abruptly threw her a brief grin.

'OK. But tie a line round yourself. And then go and tell Neil to turn the boat round. I'll try and pull Graham to the ladders on the stern.'

Thankful to be able to help, Gill obeyed. Emerging from the cabin again, she realized the need for the line around her body when another gigantic wave hit *Melinda*, as Neil began to swing the boat around. Gill was thrown off her feet, feeling herself roll helplessly towards the safety of the rail.

It was a mad world of blue-green

frothing danger; of slapping, screaming noise; of Pete's voice yelling over the uproar: 'Graham, make that line fast. We're pulling you round to the stern ladders . . . '

When she got up, she saw Graham's terrified face being battered by the waves, lifting, sinking — heard his shriek of despair as he was pulled towards the stern of the boat, where a ladder plunged and lifted as *Melinda* danced in the teeth of the storm.

' . . . Can't swim! Drowning — please help — help me . . . '

Gill knelt beside Pete at the stern, tense and shocked.

'Why doesn't he grab the ladder?' she shouted and Pete cursed in reply.

'Because he's useless! Can't do a thing to help himself, not even now — '

'I'm going to climb down and give him my hand to pull him in . . . ' She couldn't just stay there and watch him drown.

Pete jerked her back as she started to move. 'Stop it, you little fool! You'll both be lost, that way.'

'But Pete — you can't just let him drown. You can't . . . '

They were staring at each other's anguished faces, and she saw an agony of indecision cloud his eyes. The moment seemed to go on and on, even as *Melinda* bucked beneath them, and Graham's screams were lost in the wildness of the wind and water.

Then, at last, Pete's face changed. His lips moved, but she couldn't hear the words. Suddenly, going over the side, feet clambering for the rungs of the ladder, one arm stretching out as he climbed down as far as safety would allow. His voice came flying back to her over the nightmare of sound.

'Hang on, Graham. I'll get you. Don't worry, mate — just hang on a bit longer . . . '

★ ★ ★

Five minutes later it was all over. *Melinda*'s engines revved and she turned again, this time heading for home. Down in the stateroom Graham lay in a waterlogged heap, still gasping, but colour slowly returning to his face, as he managed to swallow sips of warming spirit. Beside him, Gill chafed his icy hands, bundled blankets about him, and smiled reassuringly.

'You're safe now. It's all over. Pete saved you. Oh, Graham, he got you onto the ladder just in time. You wouldn't have lasted much longer . . . '

Feebly, Graham nodded. 'I know. Good old Pete. Who'd have thought it — saved me, eh? And after I was too yellow to do the same for his dad, when he was in the water . . . '

Pete came down the steps, to crouch over Graham. 'So you finally admitted it. Well, I was right, then. I always knew it was your fault Dad drowned.'

He stared at Graham with hard, thoughtful eyes, and Gill held her breath. Then, unable to stand the mounting tension, she slipped her hand into Pete's, and made him look at her.

'Thank you,' she whispered unevenly. 'Thank you for saving him. And — for forgiving him, too . . . ' She began to tremble, with cold, and with shock, but mostly with fear of what Pete's reaction would be to those last words.

Slowly, his face relaxed. He pressed her hand until she could have screamed — but it was joy that filled her, not pain, as he added, very gently, 'Yes, I have forgiven him. Didn't think I could, but when I saw him in trouble, I understood just what a killer the sea can be and Graham — like Dad — was a victim. I hadn't thought of it like that before . . . now, I understand.'

The throb of the engines lessened, and Pete lifted his head to stare up at the porthole above the long seat where Graham lay.

'We're back in harbour. Nearly home.' He smiled, first at Graham, and then at Gill, a long, lingering smile that made her feel dizzy with happiness. 'Home from troubled waters,' he said and touched her cold face in a gesture that spoke for itself.

* * *

Those few words remained in her mind during the aftermath of the accident, a bedrock of security and hope, as things gradually returned to the routine of normal living. By the end of the week further trials — in better weather — established that *Melinda II* was seaworthy. Neil ferried her over to France, with Brigitte and Graham flying out to be in port when Monsieur Leconte finally took possession of his boat.

After so much drama it seemed improbable that life could settle down, but it did. Gill returned to her office and Pete to the yard, where a new keel of the approved type was laid down for the newly-commissioned luxury cruiser. The Wayland story, it seemed, would progress favourably, from now on.

Some weeks later Gill, wandering on

the beach one evening, wondered at the serenity of the tiny waves lapping at her feet as she walked along the littered tideline.

Her mind was so full of remembered images and voices that Pete reached her before she knew it.

His arms halted her slow progress, and he smiled down into her startled face with a vivacity and resolution that reminded her of the younger man she had known and loved even then.

'I've been too busy working to talk to you, lately,' he said wryly. 'And too busy thinking to come and find you, after work. Thinking about us, Gill, love . . . '

She waited. No more for her the foolish impetuosity of making demands, of seeking changes, or of trying to manipulate events and people. Like the elements, she had learned to just let things happen.

Pete was smiling gently as he linked an arm through hers and swung her around, heading for his distant cottage at the far end of the long, curving beach.

'Care for fish-fingers?' he asked innocently, and she nodded, reading in his eyes the message that she sensed would be made quite clear before the night was out.

Home from troubled waters, indeed.

THE END

Other titles in the Linford Romance Library

SAVAGE PARADISE
Sheila Belshaw

For four years, Diana Hamilton had dreamed of returning to Luangwa Valley in Zambia. Now she was back — and, after a close encounter with a rhino — was receiving a lecture from a tall, khaki-clad man on the dangers of going into the bush alone!

PAST BETRAYALS
Giulia Gray

As soon as Jon realized that Julia had fallen in love with him, he broke off their relationship and returned to work in the Middle East. When Jon's best friend, Danny, proposed a marriage of friendship, Julia accepted. Then Jon returned and Julia discovered her love for him remained unchanged.

PRETTY MAIDS ALL IN A ROW
Rose Meadows

The six beautiful daughters of George III of England dreamt of handsome princes coming to claim them, but the King always found some excuse to reject proposals of marriage. This is the story of what befell the Princesses as they began to seek lovers at their father's court, leaving behind rumours of secret marriages and illegitimate children.

THE GOLDEN GIRL
Paula Lindsay

Sarah had everything — wealth, social background, great beauty and magnetic charm. Her heart was ruled by love and compassion for the less fortunate in life. Yet, when one man's happiness was at stake, she failed him — and herself.

A DREAM OF HER OWN
Barbara Best

A stranger gently kisses Sarah Danbury at her Betrothal Ball. Little does she realise that she is to meet this mysterious man again in very different circumstances.

HOSTAGE OF LOVE
Nara Lake

From the moment pretty Emma Tregear, the only child of a Van Diemen's Land magnate, met Philip Despard, she was desperately in love. Unfortunately, handsome Philip was a convict on parole.

THE ROAD TO BENDOUR
Joyce Eaglestone

Mary Mackenzie had lived a sheltered life on the family farm in Scotland. When she took a job in the city she was soon in a romantic maze from which only she could find the way out.

NEW BEGINNINGS
Ann Jennings

On the plane to his new job in a hospital in Turkey, Felix asked Harriet to put their engagement on hold, as Philippe Krir, the Director of Bodrum hospital, refused to hire 'attached' people. But, without an engagement ring, what possible excuse did Harriet have for holding Philippe at bay?

THE CAPTAIN'S LADY
Rachelle Edwards

1820: When Lianne Vernon becomes governess at Elswick Manor, she finds her young pupil is given to strange imaginings and that her employer, Captain Gideon Lang, is the most enigmatic man she has ever encountered. Soon Lianne begins to fear for her pupil's safety.

THE VAUGHAN PRIDE
Margaret Miles

As the new owner of Southwood Manor, Laura Vaughan discovers that she's even more poverty stricken than before. She also finds that her neighbour, the handsome Marius Kerr, is a little too close for comfort.

HONEY-POT
Mira Stables

Lovely, well-born, well-dowered, Russet Ingram drew all men to her. Yet here she was, a prisoner of the one man immune to her graces — accused of frivolously tampering with his young ward's romance!

DREAM OF LOVE
Helen McCabe

When there is a break-in at the art gallery she runs, Jade can't believe that Corin Bossinney is a trickster, or that she'd fallen for the oldest trick in the book . . .

FOR LOVE OF OLIVER
Diney Delancey

When Oliver Scott buys her family home, Carly retains the stable block from which she runs her riding school. But she soon discovers Oliver is not an easy neighbour to have. Then Carly is presented with a new challenge, one she must face for love of Oliver.

THE SECRET OF MONKS' HOUSE
Rachelle Edwards

Soon after her arrival at Monks' House, Lilith had been told that it was haunted by a monk, and she had laughed. Of greater interest was their neighbour, the mysterious Fabian Delamaye. Was he truly as debauched as rumour told, and what was the truth about his wife's death?

THE SPANISH HOUSE
Nancy John

Lynn couldn't help falling in love with the arrogant Brett Sackville. But Brett refused to believe that she felt nothing for his half-brother, Rafael. Lynn knew that the cruel game Brett made her play to protect Rafael's heart could end only by breaking hers.

PROUD SURGEON
Lynne Collins

Calder Savage, the new Senior Surgical Officer at St. Antony's Hospital, had really lived up to his name, venting a savage irony on anyone who fell foul of him. But when he gave Staff Nurse Honor Portland a lift home, she was surprised to find what an interesting man he was.

A PARTNER FOR PENNY
Pamela Forest

Penny had grown up with Christopher Lloyd and saw in him the older brother she'd never had. She was dismayed when he was arrogantly confident that she should not trust her new business colleague, Gerald Hart. She opposed Chris by setting out to win Gerald as a partner both in love and business.

SURGEON ASHORE
Ann Jennings

Luke Roderick, the new Consultant Surgeon for Accident and Emergency, couldn't understand why Staff Nurse Naomi Selbourne refused to apply for the vacant post of Sister. Naomi wasn't about to tell him that she moonlighted as a waitress in order to support her small nephew, Toby.